LET'S HEAR IT FOR THE BOYS!

A HitLitPro Anthology

Published in 2014 by
ThornBerry Publishing UK
in conjunction with
CandleLit Author Services
in aid of Movember.

CandleLit
Author Services

All royalties donated to the Movember Foundation

ISBN 978-1-909734-265

Also available in Ebook format

ThornBerry Publishing UK,
South Gloucestershire, England

No part of this publication may be reproduced, copied, stored in a retrieval system, or transmitted, in any form or by any means, without the prior written consent of the copyright holder, nor be otherwise circulated in any form of binding or cover other than that in which it is published and without a similar condition being imposed on the subsequent purchaser. All images are the property and copyright of the authors and/or publisher and may not be reproduced in any media without written permission.

Disclaimer

Dedication

Mo Sistas, it's time to step up...

Perhaps one of the men close to you (brother, husband, son, friend...) join in with the moustachioed adventure that happens every November. Around the world it's the month that has literally changed its name, as the global organisation, Movember, leads the way in changing the face of men's health.

This year it is time for the ladies to step up and grab the moustache baton. While we Mo Sistas may be follicly challenged about the face, we do have the power of words at our fingertips.

Let's Hear It For The Boys is a tribute to the men of Movember. The HitLitPro authors have created these nine short stories to celebrate the men in our lives, the effect they have on our hearts, our minds (and our bodies), and the difference they can make to the world around them.

CONTENTS

FOREWORD

Of all the charitable initiatives out there, Movember is one that is closest to many people's hearts. Not only is it a matter of joining a global community and working towards a worthwhile aim together, it encompasses the new and the old in order to protect the future. The mere concept of asking men to grow moustaches – often itchy and sometimes bizarre-looking – is an unusual one, but Movember goes much further than this. The true spirit behind Movember is perfectly summed up in their 4th and 5th Rules:

Rule 4: Use the power of the moustache to create conversations about men's health and to raise funds for prostate cancer, testicular cancer and mental health.

Rule 5: Each Mo Bro must conduct himself like a true gentleman.

(A full list of rules can be found on the Movember website: uk.movember.com.)

If ever there was a reason to start a worthy conversation, it is the appearance of an unexpected moustache. And to start that conversation in this manner is so effective because it frames it in a positive light, focusing on the progression towards awareness and ultimately a cure. And Rule 5 touches at the very crux of the matter, casting our minds back to a near-forgotten era of moustachioed men in tailcoats, holding doors open for ladies.

Perhaps it is through rose-tinted glasses that we look back, but it is this quality that we all hold so dear to our hearts. The men with unwavering principles; charm without arrogance; the willingness to put themselves out for others. These are the men that we admire and stand by with unwavering loyalty, and it is to these men that the Hit Lit Pro authors have dedicated *Let's Hear It For The Boys*.

Each story in this anthology is a testament to these men and the stories they carry around with them, shaping them as individuals and as gentlemen. The Hit Lit Pro authors offer stories with a timeless quality that capture the essence of what makes the men in our lives so very special. Due to their nature, short stories need to hold a value that novels do not, and this anthology offers just that. It is like dipping into a box of chocolates; eager for a taste of something divine and knowing it will leave you wanting more.

As a whole, this collection offers romance, reflection and men that you can't help but adore (moustachioed, bearded and unshaven alike). They are stories about love and the effect others have on us, for better or worse; about meeting strangers and letting them unleash something within us; about the sacrifices we make for those closest to our hearts; and about looking back on the lives we once had and recapturing a little of that vitality. Written for those of us who still believe there is something more than just "okay".

Read this anthology all at once, or dip into it as and when your heart needs a little warming; the choice is yours. And if you like what you read here, then please explore the multitude of bestselling novels available from the Hit Lit Pro authors.

by **Elizabeth A. Wright**
CandleLit Author Services

MOVEMBER FACT FILE

Prostate Cancer

- In Britain alone, over 40,000 men are diagnosed with prostate cancer EVERY year.
- 13% of cancerous male deaths are due to prostate cancer. That's one death every hour in the UK.
- The risk increases with age.
- 1 in 8 men will be diagnosed at some point in their lifetime.
- The prostate is the gland below the bladder which enriches sperm.
- Poor diet, lack of exercise and genetics can play a part in the onset of prostate cancer.
- Only when advanced will symptoms, such as difficulty getting an erection, urinary issues and blood in urine or semen, be apparent. It is better to be tested before.
- There are two easy tests: blood tests and a physical exam, and if you are diagnosed during early stages the outlook is often still positive.
- Prostate Cancer UK (PCUK) is the biggest men's health charity.
  Find more information at: prostatecanceruk.org.

Testicular Cancer

- In 2011, 2,200 men were diagnosed with testicular cancer.

- It is the most common cancer diagnosed in men between the ages of 25–49.
- It is generally rare in non-Caucasian men.
- Incidence of testicular cancer has nearly doubled since the 1970s in the UK...
- ...but survival rates have risen. The current rate is 95%.
- Testicular cancer commonly presents itself as a small, hard lump in one or both testicles. Other symptoms can include: abdominal pain, a change of size or shape of the testicles, breast tissue tenderness or swelling and a sudden build-up of fluid in the scrotum.
- The causes are unclear, but possible factors in the onset of testicular cancer could be: undescended testes at birth, and a family or personal history of cancer.
- Testicular self-examination is essential in spotting signs of cancer. You can find guides online.
- Orchid Male Charity Cancer is a Movember supported charity. For more information visit: www.yourprivates.org.uk.

Mental Health Problems

- The five main mental health problems affecting men in the UK are: depression, anxiety, bipolar disorder, psychosis and schizophrenia and eating disorders.

- Anxiety mixed with depression is the most common.
- 1 in 8 men are diagnosed with a mental disorder at any one time.
- In 2011 there were 6,045 suicide deaths in the UK. 75% were male.
- The highest suicide rate is men between 30–44.

Due to a lack of awareness, a sense that mental disorders are not "manly", or risky avoidance behaviours, mental disorders in men often go undetected. Anyone can be at risk from mental disorders but stress, substance abuse or traumatic events can often trigger their onset.

For more information Movember suggests:
NHS: www.nhs.uk/NHSEngland
Mind: www.mind.org.uk
Papyrus: www.papyrus-uk.org
Calm: www.thecalmzone.net
Samaritans: www.samaritans.org

LET'S HEAR IT

FOR THE BOYS!

A CHANCE ENCOUNTER
by Sheryl Browne

She hadn't even wanted to go to Adam's office party. Hoping her mind might drift into neutral, Joanne idly studied the graffiti merging into one glorious multi-coloured snake, as the train hurtled out of the station. Absolutely nothing in her wardrobe that could be considered remotely trendy, she'd almost feigned illness at the last minute. Her failsafe Dior LBD had been her last hope. Backless, and slim-fitting, it might have looked stunning, if only she could have walked backwards. She seemed to have put on a stone overnight.

No, not overnight, she conceded. She'd struggled to lose the weight after her miscarriage. She'd felt fat and frumpy and unattractive. Why bother, she'd wondered, skipping the gym in favour of chocolate and wine. Date nights seemed almost to have slipped off the agenda too, work demands and those of two warring teenagers sapping her energies. She loved her kids, with her very bones, but sometimes lately, exhausted by being the linchpin around which house and home pivoted, Jo had found herself longing for a little "me" time, where she would be able to tend to her own needs, rather than those of her family. She'd had plenty of time to herself last night. And she'd hated every lonely minute of it.

Jo swallowed, feeling the tears she'd finally given in to brimming afresh. All alone in an unfriendly hotel room, she'd sobbed until she thought her heart might break, until she'd retched dry tears and simply couldn't cry any more. She'd grieved the loss of her husband as surely as if Adam were dead.

Jarred from her thoughts, Jo tried to ignore the man hesitating in the gangway beside her. *Please, please, sit somewhere else*, she prayed silently, hoping he'd move on, and feeling immensely relieved when he did. Normally she'd smile and try to be sociable. Other people had life problems to deal with, she often reminded herself, so why not try to spread a little cheer? Not this time though.

Jo didn't feel like smiling today.

What she'd quite like to do was smoke a cigarette, which she hadn't done for years. It was because she was on the train, she supposed, taking the same journey she had in her uni days, untroubled by life; the world her oyster, as free as a bird to do what she wanted, to go where she wanted. She'd got lost somewhere along the way. She wasn't sure where. Studying her watery reflection in the window, Jo didn't recognise the woman looking back.

She'd met Adam at uni. Two years older than her, he'd been quiet, studious, and bone-meltingly good-looking. With his rugby-player's honed physique and dark, decadent chocolate brown eyes, she'd fancied him immediately. She'd fallen for him hard; loved him, all of him, completely. And now...

Jo gulped back the jagged pieces of her heart, which seemed to have settled like broken glass in her windpipe. She felt bereft, as though part of her had been torn physically from her. He'd wanted her forgiveness, begged her to come home. Left how many messages on her mobile? Jo had stopped counting. It was the lies that hurt most; the broken trust. Could Adam, or any man, ever truly understand that?

"Excuse me?" A male voice cut across her meanderings.

Jo turned distractedly towards him. "Sorry?"

"Do you mind if I...?" The same man who'd paused a moment ago indicated the seat next to hers, his eyes meeting Jo's, as he did. Striking, electric blue eyes, Jo noticed, a smile dancing therein, rather than the agitation she might have expected to see, since she'd obviously placed her overnight bag there to claim the space as her own.

"Sorry," she said again, trying to remain poised and calm as she reached for the bag. She wished she could have been that last night when she'd found Adam... Jo's heart lurched afresh at the recollection of discovering her husband, her friend, her lover, in an embrace with another woman. An embrace that left little to the imagination, and which had crushed every ounce of breath from Jo's body. Nauseated, her stomach clenching inside like a slipknot, she'd fled from the party in her ridiculous, too-tight dress, tears streaking her face and pitying looks following in her wake. Jo didn't want that. To be pitied. To be labelled a woman of a certain age, whose husband had inevitably strayed.

Adam was *her* linchpin. Jo loved him, still.

But she couldn't live a lie.

"No problem." The man smiled. And Jo wished he wouldn't, because she simply couldn't.

"Allow me," he said, reaching to relieve her of the bag, which was too big to wedge between her feet, Jo realised.

"No, I can manage," she assured him, but the

truth was, she couldn't, not without standing and moving past him. She didn't want to. Not because he was male. She was far too middle-youth to recoil at the closeness of a man. And he was clean shaven and well-dressed in his business suit, ergo obviously not the local public transport loony but, the fact was, she wanted to remain in her bubble, behind the invisible barrier she'd erected against the world while she licked her too painful wounds.

"Thank you," she relented, handing him the bag and managing a small smile.

His fingers were long, she noticed, as they closed around the handles, his hands strong, nails short and well-manicured. She'd be safe with him, she decided, settling back as, her bag now stowed on the luggage rack, he sat down beside her. He wasn't going to disturb her with muted discordance from earphones, or incessant banal conversation.

"Do you work in the city?" he asked her, and Jo's heart sank. Apparently, he was.

"No," she answered shortly.

"Oh." He nodded. Jo felt him glance at her.

Contrite, she glanced back at him.

He furrowed his brow. His bright blue eyes flick-ered back towards hers, and then he did something extraordinary for a man in a business suit on a train. He drew his thumb and forefinger across his mouth and zipped his lips.

Jo laughed, surprised, and embarrassed that this stranger could so obviously see her bad mood. "Sorry," she said.

"That's three times you've said sorry." He smiled again, a warm easy smile. "Apology accepted."

"I was shopping," she offered, by way of recompense for her rudeness.

"Ah." He nodded knowingly. "I take it you didn't save a fortune in the sales?"

"Sorr... Excuse me?"

"No carrier bags," he said, glancing upwards towards the luggage rack. "I'm assuming you didn't find many must-have bargains?"

"No. Yes. I mean..." Jo shook her head, flustered. "I was window shopping," she elaborated weakly, irked that she had to elaborate at all. Why, she couldn't help wondering, *had* he chosen that seat, rather than one of the empty ones. If he fancied his chances, it wouldn't be with her. In his early forties and undeniably attractive, he no doubt fancied himself in his prime. If he was on the "pull", he'd be after some nubile young thing to impress with his prowess, presumably. Attempting to quash this new cynicism she was feeling, Jo surreptitiously looked him over, noting the hair greying at the temples, the high cheekbones, making him textbook handsome material.

The suit was well-cut, designer, she imagined. He wore a heavy gold watch on his wrist. No ring, she noted. Yes, he would definitely be a catch. If he was single, twenty-something stick insects would kill for him. So, what was he doing making an effort at conversation with a woman whose only hope of seeing a size ten again was to look at her daughter?

"So you stayed over?" he asked, turning to her, and catching her lingering perusal of him. "In London, I mean?"

"Yes, I, um..." Jo averted her gaze "...needed some space," she mumbled, absent-mindedly twirling her own wedding band. "You know, away from incessant family demands?"

"Ah, some 'me' time," the man empathised.

"That's right." Jo tried for light-hearted, and found herself catching a sob in her throat. Swiping angrily at an errant tear that chose that moment to spill over, she pulled in a shuddery breath and looked away.

The man didn't speak for a moment, and then, "Are you all right?" he asked gently.

Jo nodded. She didn't trust herself to look at him.

"I've been over presumptuous," he said quietly. "Please accept my apologies."

Jo emitted a laugh, a rather strangulated one. "Apology accepted," she repeated his earlier comment.

"I don't have a tissue," he said, "but you're welcome to my sleeve."

Jo turned then, blinking incredulously. "I'd love to see your face if I did. That has to be made-to-measure." She nodded at his suit and reached inside her pocket for a tissue of her own.

"Armani," he supplied, shrugging indifferently. "Harrods. It's just material stuff at the end of the day, though, isn't it? Not worth much in the great scheme of things."

Blinking at him again, Jo blew as gracefully as she could.

"That was an attempt at a joke, by the way," he said, his smile rather awkward, and undeniably charming. "Material?" he added, when Jo didn't get it.

"Ah," she said, and furrowed her brow. "Oh."

He laughed. "I never did have much of a knack for making people smile."

"You made me smile," Jo assured him, "amazingly."

"Good. It suits you. You have a beautiful smile."

What? Jo searched his face sure she'd find insincerity there. There was none, a hint of sadness perhaps, but not self-assured cockiness.

"Flatterer," she scolded him, with a roll of her eyes, a blush warming her cheeks nevertheless.

"Flattery where flattery's due," he said, with a small, sincere nod.

Was he for real? Jo narrowed her eyes. It seemed he was. In which case, he would most definitely be married. If he were her man, she'd keep him tied to the headboard. Thoughts of Adam and their lovemaking, his lovemaking with another woman, immediately crowding her mind, Jo glanced back to the window.

"Oh, this stop's mine," she said, realising the train was pulling into her station.

He glanced past her. "Heck, mine too," he said, getting quickly to his feet and grabbing her bag from the rack. "Time flies..." He smiled and stood back to allow her to go before him.

"It was nice talking to you," he said, offering Jo her bag once they were on the platform. Obviously a gentleman, as well as amenable and good-looking, he'd insisted on carrying it for her. She was quite capable of carrying it herself, of course, but she'd allowed him to, indulging in the luxury of being "looked after."

"Likewise. Thank you." She smiled gratefully and reached for the bag.

He held onto it, startling Jo, whose skin tingled strangely as his fingers brushed hers. "Even if you didn't really feel like talking?" he ventured.

Jo closed her eyes and nodded. "No," she admitted. "No, I didn't, not really."

"Look, it's just a suggestion, and I won't be offended if you say no, but why don't you join me for a coffee? I have someone meeting me," he elaborated, as Jo hesitated. "My driver. I'm early though, so…"

"I don't know," Jo said uncertainly, glancing up at the old station clock. The same clock Adam would meet her under when they were courting eons ago.

"Just half an hour," he asked, with a hopeful shrug. "We could have one here." He nodded towards the quaint little railway-siding café that seemed to have been there forever. "They do a fabulous chocolate latte, and the muffins are to die for… or so I'm told." The last was said with a mischievous grin that definitely suited him.

"Okay." Jo nodded, at length. Why not, she thought. It wasn't as if she were expected home at any particular time, if at all, given the circumstances.

"Good," he said, immediately reclaiming her bag and turning towards the café. "We can keep an eye on the clock from there."

He took her arm as they walked and, oddly, Jo didn't mind. There was something about him, his demeanour, the seductive rich timbre of his voice. He seemed to lift her spirits somehow.

The chocolate latte was soothing. Matthew's conversation—he'd introduced himself on their walk there, lest she think she was about to be accosted by a strange man—was amusing, unassuming and equally soothing.

"To be honest, I thought I recognised you as someone I'd spoken to before," he answered Jo's question as to why he'd chosen to sit next to her. A spin on *haven't we met before?* Jo wasn't sure. If he was trying his luck, he wouldn't have to try very hard. She liked him. She liked the quiet reassurance that seemed to emanate from him.

"I'm married," she blurted, suddenly feeling the need to set boundaries. For him or herself, though? She was attracted to him, his easy smile, his touch, the brush of his fingertips as he'd passed her her latte, sending an undeniable fission of sexual tension the entire length of her spine. Was she really considering an intimate liaison with him, a stranger she'd just met on a train? Was he? Would she be, but for what Adam had done? She needed to be reassured, desired. Oh, and how. No one need ever know but her, she reasoned, her desire spiking at the thought of those sure hands mapping every inch of her flesh. They would be ships that passed in the night that was all. Did she truly want that? Jo didn't know. She stirred her latte thoughtfully. She was swimming in dangerous waters, and she was floundering.

"I sense not happily though?" It was more a statement than a question. His tone was cautious.

Jo shook her head, a small defeated gesture.

He hesitated, and then reached across to still her hand. Jo stopped her incessant stirring. She felt it again, that electrifying jolt. It was like nothing she'd ever experienced.

"Do you want to talk about it?" he asked, reaching for her hand as she downed her spoon, and squeezing it gently.

Jo shrugged. "Nothing much to tell," she said. "Classic scenario: wife walks into husband's office, catches husband in the act. Case closed." She shrugged again, as if it didn't hurt, as if her heart wasn't bleeding steadily inside her.

"Ah." He drew in a long breath.

Jo's eyes flicked to his.

He smiled, sympathetically but not pityingly, thank God. "Actually in the act?" he asked, after a moment.

Jo swallowed. "As good as," she assured him. "Let's just say, my timing couldn't have been better, or worse, depending on viewpoint."

He nodded slowly, trailing his thumb contemplatively over the back of Jo's hand, which played havoc with her already confused emotions. "And did you get to hear his point of view?" he asked.

Jo almost laughed. "No." She stared at him incredulously. "I didn't feel like waiting around while they adjusted their clothing. Should I have done?"

Matthew shrugged this time, his brow furrowed thoughtfully. "No," he said. "I can see why you would need to distance yourself, but ..." he glanced at her, gauging her, it seemed "...I think you do need to talk."

"Why?" Jo retrieved her hand. "To listen to his lies?"

"If he lies, then you'll have your answer."

"What answer?" Jo gauged him now.

"Whether he cares about you enough not to hurt you any further."

Jo shook her head, trying to assimilate. "But he's already lied." She didn't feel she needed to point out this obvious flaw in his defence of her adulterous husband.

"Not necessarily."

"Oh." Jo blinked at him. "So you think there's a high possibility he slipped up just the once and landed in a compromising position? With his face in the woman's cleavage and his hand up her skirt?" Her voice was loaded with sarcasm. She couldn't help it.

Matthew nodded, giving her a touché smile. "It's possible. I'm not condoning what he did, the fact that he did, or why. I'm not imagining there's a simple way forwards, but I think you do need to talk. For your children's sake," he added, causing goosebumps this time to run the length of Jo's spine.

She hadn't mentioned she had children. He'd guessed, she told herself. Obviously, she was a woman of a certain age and he'd made assumptions. Jo studied him narrowly, wondering how it was she came to be confiding in a stranger, a seemingly very perceptive stranger.

"I need some time," she said, reaching for the dregs of her latte, preferring to avoid stating whether or not she was prepared to listen to Adam's explanations, true or otherwise. "What are you anyway, a marriage counsellor?" She tried to keep her tone light, despite this man rocking her world further.

"Relate," he corrected her. "And no, but I do

11

have plenty of experience of marriage counselling."

"Oh." Jo glanced down. It took a second to digest. She almost smiled at the irony of her situation. Here she was, debating whether to leave the man who'd cheated on her, and she was sitting having casual conversation with another man who'd probably done the same to his wife. To add to the irony, she'd actually even contemplated casual sex with him.

He picked up his own spoon, fiddled with it, tugged in a long breath, and placed the spoon carefully back on his saucer. "I imagine you've got me up there on your total bastards list now?"

Jo's snapped her gaze back to his face.

"You'd be right. I am," he said, bringing his gaze slowly up from the table to meet hers. "I cheated on my wife." He closed his eyes. "I had no way to put it right. No way to undo it. I hurt her as much as any man could hurt a woman. I regretted it for the rest of my life."

Astounded at his frankness, Jo had no idea what to say.

"We grew apart," he went on, his eyes still closed, as if recollecting. "Children clamouring for attention, a bereavement: my father. I was emotionally adrift. It's no excuse. There are no excuses. I turned to another woman when I should have turned to her, the woman who knew me, who loved me, even knowing my workaholic tendencies. She needed me, too, and I wasn't there." He paused again, his eyes finally meeting hers, eyes where dark shadows now danced, Jo noticed, and far from hating him, wanting to vent her anger, as she had a second ago, her heart twisted afresh, this time for him.

"What happened?" she asked, sensing that whatever he'd done, no matter the punishment wished upon him, somehow he'd been punished enough.

"Life. Death…" He took another deep breath. It took an eternity before he breathed out. "I loved her more than any woman I'd ever loved." He stopped again, grazing a thumb across his forehead. "Sorry is such a useless bloody word, isn't it? It was all I had to offer. It wasn't enough. I lost her. I broke her trust. I broke her heart. And my heart broke a little more each day knowing how much I'd hurt her."

Jo studied him, hard. "Why are you telling me this?" she asked.

Matthew looked back at her, his face was white, taut, the anguish etched into his features almost palpable. "Because we're human and we make mistakes," he said throatily. "I don't want you to make a mistake, Joanne. Despite our supposed intelligence, our intellectual philosophising, so often our gut instinct is right. I just want you to be guided by yours."

Glancing at the clock, he shrugged and smiled, the kindness, tinged by sadness, back in his haunting blue eyes. "You need to go," he said, as the thought crossed Jo's mind.

Jo nodded. He caught her hand across the table. "I'm not supposing you do, but if you'd like to see me again," he said, and stopped.

Jo glanced away. She had no idea what to say. What her feelings were.

"Look, take my business card," he said, reaching into his inside pocket and offering one to her. "Call me if you need to. For my part," he gave her that hopeful smile again, "I'll be here next week, same time, under the clock. If I don't see you… Well, I'll be wishing you luck."

Jo had never noticed the flower stall at the station before. "A rose for your love," the flower-seller said, offering Matthew a single red rose as they walked to the station exit. Matthew bought it, paying the pleased flower-seller handsomely.

"You're a beautiful woman, Joanne," he said, handing the rose to her. "Next time you glance at your reflection, open your eyes. See what others see."

His kiss was gentle, soft, exploring, lingering. And when he looked at her, his eyes seemed to reach right down into her very soul. "Trust your instincts, Joanne," he said, once again catching hold of her hand. Trailing his thumb over her ring finger, he gave her one last heart-wrenching smile and then turned towards the exit. Would she see him again, Jo wondered, unless perchance on a train?

The house was empty when Jo arrived. She hadn't expected anyone to be home, but her attention was immediately snagged by the handwritten note taped to the kettle.

Tried to contact you, it read. *At the hospital with Luke. Adam. xx*

Jo's heart stopped dead in her chest.

He's OK!! Please don't worry. Adam had scrawled underneath, as if as an afterthought. Because he would have thought, Jo knew. He would have realised at the sight of the word hospital, that she would be wretched with worry.

Swallowing back a fresh wave of nausea, the stomach-churning guilt that threatened to overwhelm her, Jo scrambled in her bag for her mobile, calling a taxi, before checking the messages Adam had left her. There were many, the first few begging her to call him, the rest: a running commentary on her son's progress. He could have left it at the message telling her Luke had been injured on the rugby field. He could have left it there, knowing her imagination would run riot and that she would have come home. He hadn't. He'd kept her informed, every X-ray they'd taken, every test they'd carried out, every message he'd sent underlining the fact that her fourteen-year-old boy wasn't irretrievably broken. The last simply reading: he's conscious and cracking jokes.

Adam met her in reception, his face flooding with relief when he saw her.

"How is he?" Jo could barely get the words past the tight lump in her throat.

"Bruised ribs, broken femur; other than that, nothing damaged but his pride, so he tells me. How are you?" Adam scanned her eyes, his own peppered with anxiety and uncertainty. "Stupid question," he laughed ironically at his own absurdity and glanced down.

Jo drew in a breath. "Not great," she said.

Adam nodded and raked a hand through his hair. "Jo, I—"

Jo drew in another deep breath. "I need to see,

Luke, Adam."

"Of course you do." Adam nodded again, sighing heavily as she walked past him. "There are no excuses, Jo. I know that," he said, behind her, stopping her in her tracks. "I'm not going to try to offer any. I know I've hurt you, broken your trust. I know it can't be easily fixed."

Goosebumps rising again on the nape of her neck, Jo turned slowly back.

"I just wanted you to know that whatever happens, whether you go or stay, whether I go... I'll spend the rest of my life regretting it, Jo. It's an inadequate word, I know that too, but I am so bloody sorry."

Jo stared at him, seeing the dark shadows in his liquid brown eyes, the palpable anguish. The same gut-wrenching anguish, she'd seen in another man's eyes.

"I love you, Jo, more than I've ever loved any woman, or ever will. I don't want to lose you. Can we talk? Please?"

Jo swallowed and nodded. She didn't smile. She wasn't ready to do that. Not yet.

His mobile number hadn't been recognised. She didn't know how, but Jo knew, even before the awkward pause when she'd asked for him at his office, that he wouldn't be there.

She knew he wouldn't be under the clock either. How could he be? He'd died in a railway accident, they'd told her, reluctant to say more. Jo went to the station anyway, something compelling her to.

The single red rose confirmed she hadn't been

going slowly out of her mind. It was placed on the ground, right beneath the old station clock, underneath it a card that read:

Follow your instinct. Be happy.
Love, Matthew.
XXX

The End

Sheryl Browne writes edgy, humorous, heart-wrenching modern fiction. A member of the Romantic Novelists' Association and shortlisted for the Innovation in Romantic Fiction Award, Sheryl now has six books published and has just completed her Masters Degree in Creative Writing.

Sheryl's latest book, a thriller entitled The Edge of Sanity, is garnering some fabulous five star reviews in its first weeks of publication and her previous release, Learning to Love, exploring the fragility of love, life and relationships, was written around a short story looking at bereavement in childhood, which was selected for publication in the Birmingham City University Anthology, Paper and Ink, of which Sheryl is super proud.

Website: www.sherylbrowne.com
FB: www.facebook.com/SherylBrowne.Author
Twitter: twitter.com/SherylBrowne

A MOMENT IN MOVEMBER
by Caroline James

Would Billy get better in St Lees, or would his self-imposed exile send him back to the cause of his problems?

Billy pushed the china cup to one side and with a sigh, leaned back in his chair. The coffee was terrible and he longed for a pint. He scratched at the stubble on his face and wondered how long it would take him to grow a moustache; he'd probably take this opportunity to let his beard grow too. He began to regret the bet he'd had with Max to grow a moustache during the month of November, for the charity *Movember* that raised funds and brought awareness to the changing face of men's health.

For Billy had every reason to worry about his health.

On the next table, two middle-aged women and a man gossiped endlessly. They hardly drew breath between bites of teacake and strong tea. *Too much time on their hands...* Billy thought idly.

The cafe was housed on the ground floor of a three-storey building in a row of shops on the high street of St Lees, a hamlet on the west coast of Cumbria. The walls were hung with paintings by local artists and showed scenes of mountains and waterfalls from the Lake District further inland. A glass-fronted counter was stocked with a tempting display of cakes and pastries and Billy gazed hungrily at them. He longed for a chocolate éclair.

Deciding to brave another cup of the dreadful coffee, Billy reached for the tall china pot. It helped pass the time and he had plenty of that. The chattering group on the next table studied a local newspaper, they circled paragraphs and hooted with laughter and Billy wondered what was causing so much amusement. He grimaced as he finished the drink, then stood and reached for his rucksack. It was time to walk back to the cottage and try to find something to do to fill another few hours.

Billy paid the bill and went out to the street. As he walked, he looked around at the countryside and wondered how long he'd be able to stomach it here. London felt a million miles away and it was all he could do not to head straight back. But the doctor's words kept repeating themselves… *"Billy, if you don't stop smoking and drinking you'll have a cardiac arrest and it will kill you."* Billy shook his head – so much fuss over a little episode and a few angina attacks. He felt better now and knew that he should be back at work, the PR company that he'd founded ten years ago was having a record year and it was the worst possible time to be away. He hated the countryside and felt completely out of his comfort zone; Billy was city born and bred and he longed to be back in London. His sister, Claire, had found the cottage for Billy and rented it for a month. She insisted that he recuperate, his lifestyle was out of control and he needed to give his body a break. Max, his business partner, was more than capable of running things during that time. At least he had the Internet, Billy thought, and everything wasn't completely lost in this godforsaken backwater.

The cottage lay in a sheltered dip near the golf course, a brisk walk through St Lees and along the coastal path. Billy knew that Claire had chosen it deliberately for its remoteness, as the only way to get about was on foot and he'd foolishly never learnt to drive. Billy took cabs in London and occasionally the Tube, although he hated the crowds and noise in the Underground. It was a warm day for November and as he began to climb the hill, Billy felt hot and slightly breathless; he stopped and noticed a bench on the opposite side of the road. Glancing to his left, he waited for a tractor to pass then headed for the bench and sat down. He closed his eyes and sat peacefully in the sunshine, thinking of the events that had brought him to St Lees.

"You live life in the wrong lane," Billy's doctor said. "You've already had one heart attack and these angina episodes are becoming more frequent. You're too young for all this to be happening. I recommend a month off with complete rest, some fresh air and a daily walk and for God's sake lay off alcohol and cigarettes!" His words were tough but the doctor, who was also a friend, softened his tone as he continued, "Why not find yourself a decent woman and settle down a bit? You can't keep this playboy routine going for much longer; one bad marriage and endless affairs doesn't mean they'll all be the same." The doctor was right. Billy knew this but didn't know if he wanted to change his lifestyle, after all – if the alternative was living life in God's remote waiting room, watching the sun rise and the tide ebb each day, he'd sooner go out on a high with his lifestyle in the city.

He yawned and studied his watch and contemplated staying put until the pub opened. Billy folded his arms and looked around. St Lees wasn't such a bad place, if you happened to like cutesy cottages, quaint houses and a hodgepodge of city-escapees, all playing the good life in an affluent rural community. He glanced at a house on the opposite side of the road. It had a huge garden and although overrun, he could see that at one time it had been well cared for. The position was superb and the surrounding land sloped gently down to the sand dunes, beyond which lay a long inviting beach. The building covered three floors and was in urgent need of repair. Flaking paintwork crumbled from rotting window frames and the wrought iron gates lay rusted and bent. Perfect for flats, Billy thought cynically, it should be bulldozed! He stood up and, resisting the urge to go and have a pint, made his way up the hill to the cottage.

The next morning, Billy decided to walk back to the village. He'd spent several hours on the Internet, checking on campaigns that his company was involved in, and reluctantly admitted that they seemed to be coping well without him. He decided to walk along the beach and, wrapping up well to protect himself from the sharp sea breeze, set off at a leisurely pace. The weather was pleasant and dog walkers greeted him as they passed by. An old couple, huddled together against the wind, were staring up at the house on the hill.

"That used to be the best bed and breakfast in St Lees," the old man said as Billy stopped to see what they were looking at. "We had our honeymoon there," the man added with a smile. "Shame it's derelict, it was a wonderful place. We came back for years..." He trailed off and taking his wife's arm, they continued on their way. Billy nodded to the couple and kept walking. The house should be pulled down, he thought grumpily; he hated decay. The village shops didn't lighten his mood; it was half-day closing and only the café was open. Billy was annoyed that he couldn't buy a copy of *The Times* and stomped back to the café to order coffee. The owner greeted him warmly and told Billy to help himself to the papers in the rack. Billy stirred his coffee and took a sip. He shuddered – it was still terrible! He reached for a paper and pulled out a copy of the local rag, which was folded in half and had rings around sections of text. Billy realised that he was reading a lonely-hearts column and remembered the women and the man laughing the previous day. So that's what they get up to in St Lees! He glanced at the column and read with mild interest: *"Ex-townie, female, mid 40s, musician, seeks knight in shining armour to realise rural dream..."* Must be mad, Billy thought. Who would want to settle here, let alone entertain a relationship? His own marriage had crumbled three years ago and despite many flings, the only relationship Billy wanted was with his work. He stuffed the paper in his rucksack and stomped out. It had begun to rain and shaking his head, Billy fastened his jacket and hurried back to the cottage.

The days passed slowly and Billy yearned to get

back to London. He spent his time online, keeping up with friends on social networks, assuring them that he would be back in action very soon. He also ploughed through his reading list, compiled by Claire, who'd loaded Billy's iPad with books she thought suitable for recuperation. Billy became a fan of daytime TV and found that the hours soon slipped by once he was ensconced on the sofa with his feet up. His daily walks got longer and he had to admit to himself that the fresh air and healthy diet were doing him good.

A farmers' market was held in the village each Thursday and Billy enjoyed heading down there to see what the local artisans had on offer. He occasionally treated himself to a loaf of malt bread and a slab of cheese. He loved all the stalls; the colourful variety of fresh produce reminded him of Borough Market – a taste of home. This was his final time at the market, one more day to go! Billy felt quite light-hearted; the end was in sight and he'd soon be returning to London.

The market was set in a cobbled square in the centre of the remains of the Norman castle in St Lees, and Billy could hear the buzz of traders echo round the crumbling stone walls. Someone was playing a guitar and singing a folk song. It sounded quite pleasant and Billy decided to get a drink and stop for a while. The sun was warm in the sheltered courtyard of the castle and Billy chose a table and sat down. He ordered a glass of cider; one drink wouldn't do any harm, he thought as he sighed happily and took a sip. Oh for a cigarette! Billy drummed his fingers on the glass-topped table and tried to take his mind off his cravings. He shrugged off his coat and as he sat back, he imagined he was in his favourite haunt in Covent Garden.

A burst of music pierced his reverie. Billy turned to see a woman strumming a guitar with passion, her eyes were closed as she sang and she seemed lost in her music. A smile formed on her pretty face and the sun caught the highlights of her thick glossy hair, the chestnut curls bouncing on the collar of a lace blouse. Billy watched the woman with awe; she looked as if she'd found her place in the world and was at one with her choice. As the piece ended, the woman opened her eyes and stared right at Billy. The jolt he felt was wholly unexpected. He wanted to look away but was mesmerised by the gaze of her piercing blue eyes.

The woman stood up and as he finished his drink, Billy watched her pack the guitar into a case. She stretched and tucked her blouse into faded jeans. Billy admired her slender, but shapely figure.

The woman spoke. "Come on."

Billy looked around. Was she talking to him?

"Let's go for a walk," she said, and with a smile and a nod of her head indicated that Billy should follow.

Billy had no idea where he was going but his brain didn't seem capable of forming any questions. He stood up, grabbed his coat and set off behind her. They meandered through the market and he watched with interest as the woman chatted with stall holders and acknowledged people along the road. As they headed up the hill and out of the village, she stopped.

"You'll be leaving soon."

It was a statement, not a question and Billy wondered how on earth she knew.

"We've been keeping a close eye on you. You're looking well again." She reached out and touched his arm. "Shouldn't have had that cider though..." She smiled and Billy felt a warm glow permeate his body. His heart lurched and his legs suddenly felt as though they might give way. He searched round to steady himself.

"Come on, we'll sit down for a while," the woman said, and Billy realised that they were standing outside the dilapidated old house. She pulled a key from her pocket and headed through the gate.

The front door creaked as she pushed it open and stood aside. Billy walked over fallen plaster and stepped into the hallway where a mahogany banister swept round a broad staircase and sun streaked through stained-glass windows. They sat on the stairs and Billy looked through wide doors that led off to high-ceilinged rooms.

She noticed Billy's unease with the organised chaos. "It takes time to get used to things. You'll go back to the city and think everything is fine, same old routine, power lunches and targets to meet." She ran long, elegant fingers through her hair and Billy watched the soft locks curl gently on her shoulders. "But every now and then, you'll remember the calm of this village and your heart will ache. This place never leaves you." She reached out and touched Billy's arm again. "Look at me, I've taken on this old house and I've never been happier. I'm going to open a gallery, maybe do B&B, start a band – who knows?" She stood up. "You'd better walk back, you need to pack."

They strolled down the hill and she chatted all the time, pointing out landmarks on the horizon and species of birds hovering over the dunes and beach – things Billy had never noticed before.

When they reached the cottage, she stopped. "Have a safe journey, say hello to the smoke for me." The woman leaned forward and placed a kiss on Billy's cheek then turned and with a wave, jogged back up the hill. Billy touched his face. His skin tingled where she'd kissed him.

A phone rang and startled Billy out of his trance. He unlocked the door and reached for the mobile that he'd left on the living room table.

"Where've you been, you old rascal?" Max yelled, and Billy winced as he listened to his business partner rant on. "You've served your sentence," Max continued, "time to get back to work. I've organised cocktails at Pearl tomorrow night and everyone will be there; we've missed you Billy."

Billy listened to Max explain the arrangements for Billy's departure from Cumbria. A taxi would pick him up in the morning and take him to the station in Penrith, where Billy would join the London train and be back by early evening.

"How's your moustache shaping up?" Max asked. "Have you earned your money?" Max had promised to sponsor Billy for two hundred pounds if he'd grown a moustache for the Movember charity. "You've had the whole month to get it in shape, the lads in the office have grown theirs too." Max chuckled. "They look like a right bunch of reprobates…" his voice trailed off.

Billy ran his fingers over the growth on his face;

he'd grown a full beard as well as a moustache, more through idleness than in support of the worthy charity, but he quite liked the way it looked. Billy continued to listen to Max and promised to be ready the next day at 11:00 am sharp, assuring Max that he would back in London in time for cocktails. He ended the call and strolled across the kitchen to close the door, then shook his head to clear his mind. The morning felt like a dream. He remembered the woman and her forthrightness; rural life had taken on a new aspect and Billy thought that the sooner he got back to London the better!

He began to pack but as he reached for his rucksack, an old newspaper fell out and dropped to the floor. Billy bent to retrieve it.

"Ex-townie, female, mid 40s, musician, seeks knight in shining armour to realise rural dream…"

Billy stared at the words. He must be as mad as the musician! Whatever spells she'd cast were well and truly broken. He certainly wasn't a knight in shining armour; thank goodness he'd be getting back to reality tomorrow!

The following morning, Billy was ready by nine o'clock and placed his bags by the door of the cottage. He felt no sentiment as he locked up. With plenty of time to spare, he thought that he'd have a wander down to the village and pick up a paper for the journey. Probably stop and have a coffee too, by which time his taxi would be on its way. His mind bustled with new business ideas and he rubbed his hands together as he walked; he couldn't wait to get back! He found a seat at a corner table in the café and ordered a last pot of the terrible coffee before leisurely opening *The Times* to the business section. Billy's eyes bulged and he gasped as he read the headline: "*IT Expert, Kate Hemmingway, founder of Technology International, steps down...*" A studio portrait of the farmers' market musician in a smart city suit stared back. Her chestnut locks bounced on the collar of her crisp white shirt.

Billy looked around the café and out through the windows to the high street, where the place was alive with smiling faces and folk going about their day-to-day business in a happy and relaxed manner. The guitar playing female's words suddenly came back to him: "*This place never leaves you...*"

Billy mechanically poured his coffee and took a sip. The flavour hit his palette and he looked at the dark frothy liquid with surprise – it was delicious! As Billy paid his tab, the café owner asked him how he'd liked the new coffee range. Billy praised the drink then hurried out onto the street. He raced up the hill to the old house.

The door was open. Billy stepped into hallway and, still holding his newspaper, picked his way over the fallen plaster. He heard a scraping sound in a room at the back.

She stood by a window, working on a sill. The warm winter sun streamed over her face and Billy watched her rub sandpaper over the wood as she stared out at the expanse of beach below. He coughed tentatively and she turned. A wry smile re- placed the dreamy look on her face as she took in his confusion.

"Ah, I hoped you'd call by. There's a room up- stairs that's half decent if you've changed your mind," she said and held out her hand. "It's not up to London standards, though I'm sure you'll find us welcoming enough."

Without sparing a thought for the taxi that was winding its way carefully up the hill to the cottage, Billy took Kate's hand.

"The moustache has to go though." Kate smiled again and led him up the stairs.

Billy didn't hesitate. He smiled too as he followed. He suddenly felt better than he had in years and allowed himself to be engulfed in the warmth of future possibilities as a wave of happiness and well-being flooded through his rejuvenated veins.

The End

 **Caroline James** lives in Cheshire and spends her time writing romantic comedy novels, climbing mountains, and running a consultancy business. She is a member of the Romantic Novelists' Association, the Society of Authors, and a feature editor and contributor for an online magazine. Caroline writes short stories and contributes articles to many publications.

Her debut novel, *Coffee, Tea The Gypsy & Me*, is set in North West England in a country house hotel at the time of a famous gypsy horse fair. The book went straight to number three on Amazon and was Ebook of the Week in *The Sun*.

Her second novel, *So, You Think You're A Celebrity...Chef?*, is set in London, Ireland and Barbados, with much of the action taking place at an annual Gourmet Food Festival. The story takes a light-hearted and often hilarious look at the world of celebrity chefs as they battle it out for fame and fortune led by media agent Hilary Hargreaves and her team; described by one reviewer as: "AbFab Meets MasterChef in a Soap..."

Caroline's third novel will be published in 2014.

Website: www.carolinejamesauthor.co.uk
FB: www.facebook.com/carolinejamesauthor
Twitter: twitter.com/CarolineJames12

CHAMPIONS
by Emma Calin

I had two champions in my life. One was a true champion. The other was a champion of truth.

It started outside a cafe. We never said it the French way. To us it was a "Kaff". It was in that strange no man's land of the early sixties when the motorcycle chains of our imaginations stretched as far as the moon. The universe beyond was still the kiss of a girl's lips and a jukebox Brylcreem-slicked with Rock and Roll.

Her name was Sheila White. Her calves were sculpted by her black patent stilettos. I was a powerless kid. She was controller of the world. We were seventeen.

They hung out at the Fourways Cafe. Their bikes were lined up on the road outside, their metal still hot, pinking and creaking from the roar of battle with tarmac. Oil dripped from engines like the blood of knights fresh from the slaughter of dragons except that it was 1962.

She worked at the meat pie factory and lived at the far end of my street. She walked by every day. She went out with a biker called Mitch. He had a skull tattoo on his hand, a leather jacket and a 1959 Triumph Speed Twin motorcycle. He was a collection of everything I wanted. The lovely arms of Sheila White folded around his waist as she clung to his speeding bike in her tight ice-blue jeans. One day I would kiss her and say her name *Sheila, Sheila, Sheila* over and over until there was just a blurred mix of her and me. One day I would dare to enter the Fourways Cafe. One day I would speak to

32

Sheila White. One day she would speak to me.

That Friday evening, I bought a new pair of jeans. Not dark-blue but ice-blue. It put me in a club. Only Rockers and Greasers wore ice-blue. It wasn't cool. It was a step outside. I tried them on in the shop and didn't take them off. I was wearing my working donkey-jacket and my under-vest. My route took me past the Fourways Cafe. The bikes were lined up outside. A guy had just pulled up and was revving his engine. A couple of others ambled out. My heart pounded. There, leaning against the wall, was Sheila White. She flicked her cigarette end out into the street. I watched it as if it were a holy relic, bearing her red lipstick and the sweet juices of her mouth. I slowed and casually pulled out a pack of cigarettes. It was a strange feeling because I didn't smoke or really know how. I'd bought a pack of Capstan Full Strength. The TV advertisements explained that only the toughest men were equal to their power. I realised I hadn't got any matches. Too bad – I'd have to just dangle it between my lips. I pulled up the collar of my coat and walked on. I knew the Rockers were watching me and I couldn't hesitate. What mattered was that she saw my ice-blue jeans, knew that I had come over to her side. I would just walk by, then half turn with a tough guy Hollywood smile.

The guys were blocking the pavement.

"We in your way, mate?" said one, grinning and combing back his oily hair.

The others laughed. This was not going to plan. I was a big lad, working as a driver's mate at the brewery, loading trucks. I didn't have the nature for fights.

"Looks like you want to be," I said, hoping the fearful dryness of my mouth didn't show.

"Looks like you're shitting yourself," said the Rocker.

There was more laughter. If I failed here my chance with Sheila White would be gone forever. I'd never be able to touch her hair or hold her to me telling her she was an angel, or any of the things I dreamed of with her.

"Guess you know more about shit than me," I said.

No one laughed. Couldn't they see I'd gone to ice-blue? I was leaving my old life and friends behind; not that I had many friends. Over his shoulder I saw Sheila look towards me. I caught her eye. A warm flood of joy swept through me. She had noticed me.

"You wanna light for that fag?" said one of the others. He had gone to her side and placed an arm around her waist. This was Mitch. His hair was night black and slicked back in a pure slippery symmetry. He was beach-master sea-lion. This was true living grease.

I stepped past the first guy and accepted the smoky flame from his Ronson lighter. This was it. I knew her eyes were on me. I took a drag and tried to inhale. The street reeled and swayed. I fought back vomit. I kept myself upright.

"Thanks."

"You gotta bike?" said Mitch.

"Yeah."

"What is it?"

"Triumph Bonneville 650," I said.

"I ain't never seen you on it," said a strangely

sharp female voice.

Time stopped. She had spoken to me.

"Didn't know you'd ever seen me," I said.

I watched her mouth shaping her reply. Her two front teeth were slightly crossed. It made her just a little human but no less angel. I loved her more.

"I'd notice anyone on a Bonneville," she said.

"Where's this bike, then?" asked Mitch.

"In Oakley's bike shop. I gotta pick it up next Saturday."

"Make sure you bring it straight round here. We'll do a ton down to the Chequered Flag Cafe," said Mitch.

I nodded in a tough-guy Brando-Waterfront way. I might have looked a bit stupid. He looked me up and down. He took in the ice-blue jeans and sauntered back into the cafe. I looked up to find Sheila's eyes on my face, staring back at me from the door. There was a slight question in her expression. I gave her the moody movie-star smile and turned away. Behind me I heard the jukebox blare out Elvis singing "She's Not You". I sang along. The King knew that truth. No one else in this world was *her*.

"Jimmy, why you wearing those?" said my mum as I walked in.

I smiled, put a fiver down on the table and kissed her cheek. I had my wage packet in my pocket.

"You look like that lot down that bloody cafe," she said.

"I just like ice-blue."

She was frying some pig's liver with mash and cabbage for dinner.

"I hope you're not gonna be hangin' about up that fair wearing them," she said.

Of course that's exactly what I'd planned to be doing. Wally Coker's travelling amusements were built up on Streatham Common. It sounds daft but the drama and glamour of the rides were an opera to me. The throb of the big generators was the pulse of a living thing. The blaring music from the dodgem and waltzer rides filled me with dreams of being Billy Fury or one of the Tornados. I loved to look at the trucks that dragged the trailers. I dreamed of the day when I would be twenty-one and could be a big truck driver. Then I'd be hauling heavy goods, resting a tough tattooed forearm out of the cab window. I'd look down from my eight-wheeler Leyland to see Sheila White and draw her up to kiss her darling angel lips.

My dad came in and broke my daydream.

"Bloody Greaser's jeans," he said with a chuckle. Like every Friday, he'd brought in a bottle of light ale to drink with his meal and a box of chocolates for my mum. He took a big swig of beer and let out a sigh. He worked shovelling tarmac and stone on the Lambeth council road-repair gang. He always smelled of sweat at the end of the day. So did I, but my sweat was different somehow, like he was a different tribe or something. Once I'd caught my mum kinda sniffing him and saying it turned her on. I still didn't know what she meant.

"I hope you're staying away from that fair," he said.

"What is this? I've always been before. I've already told Colin I'd go with him."

Colin had been my mate since first day at school.

He worked in an ironmonger's shop and sure wasn't into ice-blue jeans or big bikes. *He* wasn't in love with Sheila White.

"Wally Coker's fair's always trouble," he said.

"They play all the latest records on the rides," I said.

"We don't want you to go," said my mum.

I shrugged. I never argued with her. I could hear in her voice she was worried and serious. All the same, I was out to work and bringing in money. I wasn't a kid. Anyway, I had bigger worries than that. I needed a motorcycle.

"How much is a Triumph Bonneville 650?" I asked.

"More money than you can afford. Must be about five hundred pounds," said my dad.

"I could put it on the never-never," I said.

"Yeah – and you'd be in debt up to your neck. Anyway, you've got a motorbike," said Mum.

That was true. I had an ex post office BSA Bantam telegram bike. Since my feelings for Sheila had developed I'd not ridden it for fear of her seeing me on a pathetic little pop-pop. That's why I walked to work and blistered my feet in my steel toe capped boots.

"I've got my full licence," I said.

My mum sighed. "I know this is all about that bloody tart."

"What tart?" I said.

"Don't be daft. That ratty lookin' girl teetering up the street on her high heels and sausage legs with a fag in her gob. You can't take your eyes off her."

"I've never noticed anyone like that," I said.

"Okay, okay, let's leave it, eh," said my dad.

He was looking over my head at my mum. I could see he was trying to stop her.

"God, why am I an only child? Why do I get all this attention?" I said.

"I couldn't have any more after you. I would have done, believe me."

Her reply was quick and volcano hot. I heard a break in her voice as if she was about to cry. I felt bad that I'd not just shut up. Dad got up from his dinner and went to her. He shot me a glance and a nod at the door. I got the message and slipped out while he held her.

What had I done?

Colin's mum made us a cup of tea before she went out to the Bingo. She'd been on her own since Colin's dad had been killed in the Korean War.

I told Colin all about my moment with Sheila White and my need for a Bonneville 650. Mainly he nodded, staring at my ice-blue jeans.

"You ain't a real Greaser, Jim," he said at last, "that girl's messed you up, mate."

"Nah, she ain't. I want a big bike just cos I like 'em."

"Your only chance is hire-purchase but you'll need your mum or dad to sign the contract. *And* you'll need a deposit of at least forty quid," he said.

I had savings of about fifteen pounds and on a good week with overtime I earned about ten quid.

Colin stopped chewing his bottom lip and looked at me as if trying to assess my character.

"There's a boxing booth at the fair and you can win twenty-five pound if you do three rounds with the champ. There's posters everywhere. You have to fight Frankie Johnson."

"What, the ex British middleweight champion?"

"Yeah, but he's older than your dad. He got tied up with some film actress. They bought a night club place and he ended up drinking the profits. He's a piss-head on the bones of his ass, Jim."

I was a heavyweight. I was the strongest labourer in the brewery. I imagined Sheila White's small soft hands touching my skin as she held my waist on the back of my Bonneville.

"I'll do it," I said.

"I'll come along at a distance. I won't admit to being with anyone wearing ice-blue jeans," he said.

We walked down to Streatham Common. It was an early autumn night. The fairground lights stood out against the darkening sky. Families were coming away and groups of young men and women were heading in, reds and blues pop-art painting their faces. Hot dog onions fizzed with stark garlic dodgem car sparks and flowed out on wheeling waltzer waves of Red River Rock on saxed-up hi-fi tracks. The diesels raised their exhaust-flaps to heaven in homage to this beauty and to Johnny and the Hurricanes. Excitement and fear pulsed through my racing heart. An angel's hand was in mine. I didn't turn to see her. She was guiding me now.

"I love you, Sheila," I said quietly.

The boxing booth was a big tent like a circus big top. A guy was outside in a tuxedo, drumming up a crowd.

"Frankie Johnson, the famous one-time champion will take on brave Ron Higgins who learned his boxing in the merchant navy. Can he go three rounds lay-deez and gen-el-men? Can he take away twenty-five smackers in his hand? Only two shillings. Can anyone beat the famous Frankie Johnson?"

For effect the barker waved a fistful of banknotes in the air. We paid our two shillings and went inside. There was a large boxing ring in the centre and a good crowd of men. There was a smell of cigarette smoke, beer breath, sweat and damp grass. Among the crowd of legs on the other side of the tent I saw the ice-blue jeans of the biker, Mitch. He was with one of the others but not *her*. He nodded an acknowledgement. I was moving up.

The tuxedo guy climbed up into the ring, followed by the fighters. The challenger wore a double-breasted suit jacket over his bare chest and shoulders without his arms in the sleeves. He was gloved-up. He wore football shorts and regular socks and shoes. He was a pale man of about forty.

Frankie Johnson wore a silk ring-gown and high-laced boxing boots. He shadow-boxed, ducked and weaved like a pro. His face was unbelievably battle-scarred. The other guy just stood limp and expressionless as if he were waiting for a bus.

A bell rang and the MC transformed into the referee. The crowd yelled and cheered for the brave challenger. The champ slapped into his white body and soon his skin was pink and red. He survived the first round. In the second the bloke lashed out at Frankie and even pushed him back against the ropes. The crowd stepped up the noise as the third round began. Maybe this poor guy from the merchant navy could survive and win the twenty-five pounds? I bellowed for him to smack the champ down to the floor. I'd been an underdog too. Every man yelling for the amateur guy had been slapped down in some way and every man there could share that shame with a kind of pride. I was learning things.

About half way through the round, Frankie Johnson came up onto his toes and started to move. The other guy looked like a hopeless mug swinging at a shadow. It looked to me as if the champ hit his shoulder but the challenger went down and stayed down. The referee returned to his tuxedo role with the microphone.

"Lay-deez an' gen-le-men – what a brave contestant. Give a big hand to Ron Higgins from the merchant navy for his courage. He very nearly made it, lay-deez and gen-el-men. Because of his pluck, lay-deez an' gen-el-men, we're gonna give Ron from the merchant navy the chance to go round with his hat. I hope you'll be generous in showing your respect for his efforts."

By this time the champ was holding up the challenger's arm in the centre of the ring. A trilby hat appeared and the defeated warrior did the rounds. It looked like everyone was putting in. I slung in another couple of shillings and so did Colin.

The MC started up again.

"There must be another man out there bold enough to show what he's worth. Come on gents – who's got the guts to step up for the next bout with Frankie Johnson?"

That other bloke had nearly got through. I was bigger and stronger than him. I had a last glance at Colin and called out.

"Over here, mate. I'll have a go."

The MC waved me over to the ring and I climbed in.

"What's your name, son? Must be a local boy? I'm guessing you're twenty-one?"

"Jimmy Paige. I work at the brewery."

"Lay-deez an' gen-el-men – our next challenger: twenty-one year old London heavyweight championship contender Billy Mason. He's a big strong boy, you'll all agree. It's gonna be one hell of a contest. Be back for the big fight in half an hour, lay-deez an' gen-el-men."

The sides of the tent were rolled up and the crowd melted away.

"I'm not any sort of heavyweight champion," I said.

"Didn't say you was, boy; anyone can hope any-thing. Punters is what we want. You'll see."

They led me through the fairground to a big four-wheeler showman's caravan away from the rides. There was a dog chained up underneath. The merchant navy guy was with us. I couldn't work out why he was there.

Once up in the wagon, the MC or referee got out a bottle of whisky. Each man took a swig. Frankie handed me the bottle. I took a long gulp. At least it was better than smoking.

"Get him sorted out," said the merchant navy challenger.

A minute later I was alone with the champ.

"You gotta be twenty-one, okay," he said in a slurred deep voice.

"I am," I said.

"You ever boxed?"

"Nah."

"Ever had a shave?"

"Yeah, a bit."

"Good. Now, here's the script. You can try and beat me. If you want it that way you'll crawl out of that ring looking for your teeth to take home to your mum. You can help me put on a show and you'll go home with a fair bit of cash."

I didn't really know what was going on. I think I sounded afraid and I was.

"I need twenty-five quid. I really need it."

"You'll get more than that. I don't want to beat you up son; but I can."

He flicked out a hand at my chin. It caught me before I could react. It was hard enough to focus me on the idea of survival.

"So how do I get any money?"

"We let you go round with the hat – you'll pick up at least forty quid."

"I thought that was a special reward for the merchant navy guy."

"You're as green as that grass, son. If there's no punter the boss steps in for the bout. The closest he's been to the navy was a trip on the Rotherhithe ferry. I shouldn't really tell you that so never let on."

I actually laughed but it probably sounded like a tremble.

He showed me how to put on the gloves and found me an old mac to put round my shoulders.

"You gotta look like a punter – some poor guy without the proper kit. I'm the big bad pro. I look the part and you look the prat. They hate me and they love you. Life's an acting job. I was right up there once, son, but this is the only script I've got for today."

I wore the same football shorts as the last guy. They fell down and he gave me a rusty safety pin to take up the slack. For the next fifteen minutes I took a boxing master-class with Frankie Johnson. He showed me how to swing and miss and how to hit the shoulder when his chin was tucked in to make it look like a knockout punch. He told me he'd mainly slap me with body punches that made a loud sound. He wanted me to take a count of seven at the end of the first round and be saved by the bell. Then I'd come out like a hero for round two and he'd back off.

We both took a good slug of whisky before going back to the ring. I felt braver after that. The reality was that he was older than my dad and I was a good three stones heavier.

"Got a girl?" he asked.

"Yeah, Sheila White," I said.

"Didn't ask her colour, son. She here?"

"Nah."

"Pity. Girls get turned on by fights. Some do anyway. The number of girls I've had after a scrap..."

"She's too gentle," I said.

He just laughed as we ducked under the ropes.

I remembered to go down at the end of the round. The champ gave me a nod and landed a good whack on the nose. I tasted blood in my mouth. I went down on one knee. The crowd were yelling and screaming for me to get up and then the bell sounded. I went back to the corner. A guy poured some cold water over my head and gave me a bucket to spit in. It looked like pure blood.

"It's nuffink. Bit of blood goes a long way, nipper," said the guy.

We came out for the second round. Things seemed a blur. I swung a haymaker punch and all I could feel was a pain in my hand. There was a wall of noise. Then he caught me with a jab under my ribs. The pain doubled me up. Frankie kinda wrestled me and growled in my ear.

"Just a reminder, son," he said.

I got the message.

The third round began. I tried to look a bit like a boxer and bounced on my toes. I kept my gloves up and jabbed out to keep him at a distance. I could see him nodding and smiling to himself. Well, he'd shown me how to do it. Then his mood changed. He gave me a look and I knew what was coming. He threw a left hook and I leaned away. It brushed my chin enough to make me dizzy. Something in my soul gave me the pride to fight to win. I was much taller. I saw him ducking in low to get inside my range. Then the lights went out. I've no idea to this day what happened. Colin told me it was an upper cut. I think it was a meteorite. I think I cried out to God that Sheila didn't have sausage legs.

Then there was cold water, smelling salts and a tour round the crowd with a trilby hat. People were patting me and calling me a hero. Money was spilling over onto the brim.

Back at the caravan we counted the take. I couldn't believe it. There was fifty-seven quid. Frankie Johnson went off for a minute and came back with a fiver and chucked it in the hat.

"That makes an even number, son. Odd numbers are unlucky. You got the skill but not the talent to be a great boxer," he said.

"What's the talent?"

"It's in the eyes, son, not the fists. There's kindness but no killer in ya. Always know you ain't got that. Be happy and live the life you can handle."

We shook hands and I walked away from the dark empty fairground. In the diesel fuel and wet grass air was the extra smell of old cooking fat and the barking of dogs. The money was wrapped up in a dirty rag. Colin was waiting for me. He was a top mate.

"Christ, you bloody near put him down in the second round," he said.

Everything was a flesh-pink buzz in my head. Sheila White's light touch soothed me for a second. I knew Colin was telling me something.

"Your dad was there. Are you listening? Did you know that?"

I tried to think. I wasn't supposed to go. Why had my dad been there?

"I got sixty quid," I said.

I think we walked home. I woke up in time to go to work. It was Saturday but you had to take the overtime when you could. I'd needed money for when I had a life with Sheila. Also I could bung a bit extra to my mum and that made me feel proud of myself. She was saving up for a holiday abroad.

I got back home at about four o'clock. My mum was listening to a play on the radio. She just smiled and I had a good strip-wash with carbolic soap at the sink. My dad came in about half-past five. He seemed happy enough. He'd been to watch football at Crystal Palace. My mum got up to make a meal.

"Why don't I treat us to fish and chips?" I said.

"That'd be lovely if you can afford it, Jim. I'll walk up with you and we'll get a pint on the way. You look at least twenty-one to me," said Dad.

I knew what was coming and why he'd said twenty-one.

"You gonna tell him about the birds and bees at last," said my mum.

"Yeah, it's time to tell him we ate the stork for Christmas dinner," he said.

We went to the White Lion in the High Road. He brought a pint over to the table. I waited for him to speak first. He was a humble bloke and not too good with words.

"Your mum didn't want you up that fair," he said.

"I know – I didn't really mean to go."

He seemed to ignore my answer.

"I understand why you went and I understand why she didn't want you to go. I ain't told her you went and I wanna be sure you'll never tell her."

"Thanks, Dad," I said.

He almost looked a bit tearful.

"Everybody has the right to know who and what they are, Jim. The truth is I *ain't* your dad."

I think my jaw dropped.

"What?"

"You asked your mum why you was an only child. She'd waited years for that question. It's an obvious one. She's only thirty-five now. She had you when she was eighteen and nothing since."

"So who is my dad?"

"Your father is Frankie Johnson. Your mother

was a fan and, well… girls get carried away with blokes like that. We ain't angels, Jim. I'd always loved her but from a distance – maybe you know how that is. Now you know why she didn't want you up that fair. She just thought you might meet. I told her not to be stupid. She said you'd know each other by instinct. Women think like that. Half of life is witchcraft to them and the other half is magic."

"So what happened?"

"One day she was at the bus stop. I could see she was sad and different to how she'd been. I put an arm out for her and she took it. She married me and I'm the dad on your birth certificate. I can't give her babies, Jim. It's something chemical."

I raked around for something profound to say. I took a long drink.

"Cod or haddock with your chips, Dad?" I said.

I've never said a word about it since and don't need to. We went to the bike shop the next weekend and I got the Triumph Bonneville 650. My dad signed the hire-purchase forms and wrote Father where it said relationship. My mum bought me a leather jacket as an advance Christmas present. I put on my ice-blue jeans and rode the Bonneville to the Fourways Cafe. I put the bike up on its stand outside and strolled in as if I just could. Like I knew who I was. Mitch was sitting alone. He nodded and I took over two teas. I offered him a cigarette.

"No girl?" I asked, ashamed I was only asking because I was gonna steal her.

He lit the cigarette.

"She's gone, mate. She's heard some Beatle band or something like that. It's blokes in suits now with mop-head haircuts. She threw away her ice-blue jeans and found some bloke with a guitar."

"You can't rely on anything," I said.

I took it on the chin. Maybe I could get a guitar. Maybe her legs were a bit plump.

"A ton's still one hundred miles per hour and always will be," he said.

"Let's go do it," I replied.

The End

Emma Calin writes steamy romance novels and gritty short stories about love and survival in the 21st century. She loves to create characters and drama set at the sharper end of society with witty and sassy heroines who overcome their circumstances to get the love they deserve. Often considered "cross-genre", Emma's books combine romance with crime, action, mystery and suspense, a dash of humour and a sprinkling of philosophy.

She has published a number of digital, audio and paperback books which are available on Amazon, iTunes, Google Play, B&N, Kobo etc and other good bookstores worldwide.

She also blogs about her dual life in Saint Savinien sur Charente in South West France, and Romsey, a market town in England. She feels extremely lucky to be able to experience the world and life through these two, very different, lenses.

Website: www.emmacalin.com
FB: www.facebook.com/emma.calin
Twitter: twitter.com/EmmaCalin

CURTAIN CALL
by Mandy Baggot

He bit into a Golden Delicious. The skin split, making that satisfying crack and crunch. It was so loud, Leah actually felt it, was transfixed. And, as he sunk his teeth further into the apple, her body reacted to every drop of juice spraying up and out of the fruit.

She pouted, turning her head to the left and holding the pose.

"And... cut!" The clapperboard came down. "Fantastic. I think that's a wrap."

Leah blew out a breath of relief. This was the fourth day of work on this thirty second commercial to promote healthy eating and she'd just about had enough.

"Thank fuck for that," Daniel exclaimed, wiping bits of apple flesh off his chin. "I'm dying for a fag. If I have to eat one more piece of fruit... I mean, it can't be healthy, can it?"

Leah didn't reply. What wasn't healthy was the amount of crap she had to do to make ends meet. But she shouldn't complain. It could be a whole lot worse. So, she had no money. So, she still lived with her dad. She had a box full of perfume thanks to a 'Summer Days' billboard campaign, and a voucher for fifty quid's worth of gooseberry juice from the trip to Hungary. Secretly, she wished it was fifty quid's worth of goulash. At least her dad would have eaten that.

But freebies from jobs wasn't exactly living the dream. Treading the theatrical boards was what she'd always longed to do. Juliet to a Romeo, a half-decent part in *The Mousetrap*. She'd had the training, she knew she was good enough, the opportunities just hadn't come. And then, when she'd managed to actually get an audition, her dad always seemed to scupper it. *It's me legs, Lea. Aww, God, now it's me back. Lea, you'll have to get me some of me pills this morning, I've run dry.*

She coughed, suddenly overwhelmed by smoke. She looked to Daniel inhaling hard on his cigarette, sucking in tar, nicotine and a hundred other poisons into his chest cavity. He was about to become one of the faces of the Government's new five-a-day initiative. With her caffeine and Kit-Kat addiction they were both a pair of fakes.

A sharp November wind whipped around Leah as she headed from the studio. She tugged the belt on her woollen coat a little tighter to ease the draught. She hoped her dad had switched the heating on early enough to take the chill off the house.

Striding on up the pavement she headed towards the bus stop and the route that would take her home. Her next assignment was tomorrow, an ad campaign for pet insurance. Just the thought of various breeds of dogs drooling over her made her depressed.

She blew out a breath. She really needed a pick-me-up this week. As that thought crossed her mind her eyes immediately flew across the road. The Lyceum Theatre. The ancient building, recently completely restored to its former glory, was where her passion for acting had come from. *Snow White and the Seven Dwarfs* when she was five.

The story was obviously the same old fairy-tale with jokes of the time thrown in, but it wasn't the actual play that had sparked something in her. It was the place itself and the ambience, the majesty of the building, the lights, the velvet drapes and the gilt on the walls. With the lustrous costumes, the songs and the laughter, Leah had been completely hooked. The very next year she'd been a junior member of the chorus line.

And then there was *Lost & Alive* five years ago. That had been a dream part. Troubled Rosalind dealing with racism when her boyfriend is killed and she's pregnant with a mixed-race baby. It had been such a challenge to get into that persona, to live and breathe that role with everything she had.

Leah crossed over the road and gazed up at the lion's head over the entrance. It was still as entrancing today as it had always been.

"Stars, hide your fires! Let not light see my black and deep desires."

It was a male voice, deep and over theatrical. Leah turned to look at its owner, slightly disturbed someone had managed to get alongside her without her noticing.

Tall, dark choppy hair, wearing jeans and a grey t-shirt. Good-looking.

"Sorry, that's from *Macbeth*, isn't it? What's that famous line from *Richard III*?"

"There isn't just one line. The whole play is brilliant," Leah stated, turning back to the poster advertising the Shakespeare play.

"You're a fan. A pleasure to meet you." He stretched his hand out to her.

Leah looked at the enthusiastic offering, debating whether to make contact.

"Sorry," he stated, removing his hand as rapidly

as it was offered. "My mum always says I'm over eager."

She couldn't help smiling then. He smiled back, showed a hint of white teeth behind the full lips.

"Are you going to see the show? Because you're too late for this performance. They started half an hour ago," Seth said.

"No, not tonight. I've got to get home."

"Husband? Boyfriend? Or dog?" Seth grinned.

"Your mum is right about you." Leah laughed. "But actually it's my dad. He's been ill since Margaret Thatcher was in power. In fact, I think he might blame her a bit."

"Trouble with his back?" Seth queried. "Had an accident that wasn't his fault?"

"You're very perceptive."

"I can do better than that." Seth closed his eyes and caught Leah's hand in his. "Let me see… You're an actress. A good one. But you're working jobs you hate because Fate's been unkind."

Leah held her breath, her heart thumping hard against her chest wall. Who was this person who already knew so much about her?

"But you don't want Hollywood and the bright lights of LA. You want theatre, the thrill and the fear of a new live audience every night."

Leah dragged her hand away and narrowed her eyes at the dark-haired man.

"I need to get home." She took a step back from the theatre, got ready to run if he made any dodgy moves.

Seth held his hands up. "Please, Leah, I'll come clean."

"You know my name!"

"I've been watching you, a lot." He stopped talking quickly. "Shit, that came out all wrong."

Leah was already running, faster than Mo Farah at the end of a 10k run.

The second she left him, Seth's shoulders sagged and he felt the exhaustion spread over him in waves. He hadn't thought it would be this hard. Of course it didn't have to be. Not if he spelt it all out straight-away when he approached people, told the truth, begged for help. But that wasn't what he wanted at all. That would be the David way, that way. He had to make this work. It was his determination to make this happen that was giving him the energy to get out of bed every morning.

The limousine pulled up alongside him, spraying leaves up from the kerb as it came to a halt. He really wished it didn't follow him around but, as he'd been banned from riding his motorbike, he didn't really have any other choice.

Seth pulled at the handle and opened the door. His father, David, was sat in the back seat and, as Seth got in beside him, he felt his father's eyes rest on him, waiting for information. He didn't want to tell him Leah had run away. Not when time was so precious. He simple shook his head.

"Seth, I think it's time we called in the big guns on this," David said.

Seth shook his head again, this time with more conviction and not an ounce of defeat.

"No. We discussed this." He turned to face David. "You're already pulling too many strings to get me the venue. That's it, Dad, that's all I asked you to do. That's all I want you to do."

He was becoming emotional and he hated that. He thumped the door panel with his fist as the driver set the car in motion.

"Listen, son…"

There were unshed tears in David's voice that had Seth turning away and looking to the window. He watched the city flipping by, the high-rises, the shops and bars, the people buzzing home, to restaurants, to visit friends and family, every second vibrant and filled up.

"Seth, I know what you want to achieve, I really do, but if we go public then…"

"No!" It was almost a primal scream of anguish. "Not yet. You promised me I could decide and I decide not yet. Not until I get Leah."

He heard his father sigh like the weight of the world was resting on top of him. He knew, in his world, it probably felt like that. So much guilt, so much helplessness. It was suffocating.

"This girl is really that good?"

Seth turned to his father then, his expression lifting, his eyes brightening. "She excelled at drama school even though she lost her mother at fourteen. She played Rosalind in *Lost & Alive* for a five night run at the Lyceum." Talking about the performance was setting him alive with goosebumps. "Mum took me to that play. I cried my heart out. She was phenomenal."

David nodded.

"Her father's ill. She's working crappy commercials and billboard campaigns. She deserves so much better." Seth set his eyes on David. "All the people I've chosen deserve more. And that's what

I'm going to give them."

Leah burst through the door of the house and leant against it, her breath catching in her throat. She'd got the bus, looking over her shoulder, surveying people getting on at every stop in case he'd followed her. It was creepy. Sneaking up on someone outside the theatre, knowing her name. She shivered, remembering how he'd held her hand. She looked at the skin, half expecting it to be tainted in some way.

"I hope that's you, Lea."

Her dad's shout had her dropping her hand back down and resting it on her chest as she came back into the moment.

"What's for tea? I could eat a scabby horse and its mother," Len called.

Leah braced herself and headed for the living room. She fixed a smile on her face and pulled at the zip on her bag as she walked in.

Len looked up from channel-hopping, stub of a cigarette hanging from his lips.

"You're smoking!" Leah exclaimed, horrified.

"Keep your hair on. I'm cutting back. Five a day keeps the doctor away and the tobacco manufacturers in business. Got to support the economy, Lea." Len let out a throaty laugh which ended in a coughing bout as he struggled to stub out the cigarette.

Leah pulled the plastic wrapper from her bag and banged it down on the coffee table. Ten green apples.

"What's this?" Len asked. He was looking at the

apples like they were foreign, unrecognisable objects.

"Fruit. Have you forgotten what it is?"

"I know what it is. Why've you bought them?"

"I haven't bought them. This was today's freebie from the job I did. Maybe if you had five of these instead of fags it would help your cough."

Len coiled his fingers around the apple bag, inspecting the contents.

"Don't you dare turn your nose up," Leah threatened. She was exhausted and trembling on the inside. All her organs seemed to be on a slow simmer, gaining pressure the more her father screwed his face up.

"I'm not. I just..." Len turned to her. "Why can't you get a nice sausage commercial or something by Danepak?"

And the simmer became a boiling frenzy. The tears were at her eyes again as every opportunity she'd given up rushed through her mind in flashbacks. Her agent sounding so enthusiastic, her having to turn it down because she didn't have time to prepare, couldn't make the audition, had to take something else because it was money in the bank. This shouldn't be her life. Working hard, long days, no satisfaction and the rest of the time a carer.

"Can't exactly make a meal out of apples." Len coughed hard again, crouching over his lap. Leah wanted to smother him, just like he'd smothered her dreams. But instead, she backed away, retreating out of the room while Len struggled for breath.

Every pace backwards and into the hallway took her closer to letting her tears fall. She quietly closed the door and, as the first drop fell from her eyes, she raced up the stairs.

She threw herself down onto her bed and let the emotion escape. Turning onto her back, still sobbing, she levelled her eyes at the old, wrinkled-edged poster on the wall. Marian Foster starring as Greta in *The Green Fields*. Her grandmother, top of the bill at the Palladium. She'd been a UK acting legend in her time, starring in shows, films – even a run on Broadway.

That was who Leah aspired to, not her lazy father or her dead mother who never worked a day in her life either. She wanted to be somebody. Not for fame or fortune but for the best parts, to learn from the greats, to give her all to a story, to immerse herself in a character.

She'd spent so long making do with adverts and walk-ons she'd almost forgotten what real acting was about. She wanted to get that back so badly.

She rolled back over onto her stomach and clutched at her pillow, drawing it close. The truth was, she always put herself last. And it wasn't Len's fault, it was her own.

Seth swigged from his bottle of water and checked his watch. Leah was late. He'd found out through charm and a few untruths that she was due at this studio at noon. Today her talents were going to be wasted on pet insurance. It was a crime. And seeing the way she'd behaved just from being outside the Lyceum last night, he knew it couldn't be all she wanted. But would she want him?

He shifted from foot to foot, juggling a group of chestnut leaves on the ground. His dad had spent the rest of last night trying to provide him with other options, different actresses he thought were right for the role. Seth had been so tired he hadn't listened. He'd played with the vegetable induced lasagne his mother had made them and let their voices just wash over him. Very soon everything was going to change.

The second the cab drew up alongside the building he knew it was Leah. He straightened himself up, screwed the cap onto his water bottle and prepared to say whatever it took.

Len had made a pot of tea before she'd even come downstairs that morning. She'd barely spoken but had nodded at his effort making. *I'll go down the Job Centre. I'll get the local paper, see what's in there. I'll give the bookies a miss*. He wouldn't do any of those things but he was trying to make her feel better. The truth was, Len was never going to get a job and, unless something changed, she was never going to make it in her chosen profession either. But it was entirely up to her. She had to make it happen if she wanted it badly enough. And she'd decided, on the cab ride over, she was going to do everything in her power to make her dream a reality. After this commercial she was going to tell her agent she was ready to reopen the door to other opportunities, projects she cared about – shows, films, programmes that meant something.

Leah paid the driver and stepped out onto the street, her hair moving with the breeze. She was full of determination. She couldn't give up, no matter what the obstacles she owed it to herself to give it a proper shot.

"Good morning. Another crisp autumn day," Seth announced.

She recognised him immediately and as the memory connected to her fleeing from him the night before, her handbag fell off her shoulder and hit the floor. The zip was undone and contents began leaking out onto the pavement.

"The second I pick my phone up out of the gutter I'm calling the police." She plucked her phone from the ground and wrapped her fingers around it. With her other hand she started collating her belongings back together, stuffing them into her bag.

"Why would you call the police on someone who's just trying to give you a job opportunity?"

Her breath mints and a lip salve fell back down to the ground.

"You're stalking me. And I'm not in the market for any job. I have an assignment, right here, as you obviously already know."

"Reading a script for pet insurance. Is that what you want?"

"Calling the police now." Leah pressed number icons on the screen of her phone. Seth put a hand on her arm.

"I saw you. In *Lost & Alive*. It moved me to tears," Seth said.

Leah looked up at him then. His voice had wavered just by saying the name of the play. Now she felt like she'd been coated in pepper. Every inch of her was suddenly on high alert, sensitised, squirming, alive.

She whispered, "Who are you?"

Seth smiled then. "I'm the person who's going to

make your dream come true."

She was holding onto her coffee mug like it was the only thing keeping her grounded. And she'd said nothing since he'd suggested the café. For now he was content just looking at her. He swallowed as the thought rolled through his mind. He had to keep this professional and it would be, but her performance wasn't the only reason Seth wanted Leah involved in this. To spend a week with her, getting to know the woman behind that heart-wrenching performance in *Lost & Alive*, finding out why she'd done nothing since when she had so much talent. He wanted to connect with her so much it almost scared him. If she didn't agree then he wasn't sure what came next. Although everybody had been handpicked for this task, he knew without Leah it wouldn't be anything like the same.

She raised her head from her drink, studying him so intently that in the end he had to break the eye contact.

She spoke. "I really needed the money from the pet insurance gig, so if you *are* just a stalker who can't get a date the usual way, now's the time to say."

He looked up and met her eyes, this time smiling. She had to admit, he was an attractive guy. But that wasn't enough to drop her guard. She couldn't gauge his age either. His short crop of dark hair gave nothing away and neither did his large blue eyes. She would have guessed mid-twenties if it wasn't for the faint lines around the perimeter of those eyes and the slight shadows beneath that gave a nod to tiredness. Thirty?

"The only stalking I've done of you before yesterday was on YouTube," he answered.

"Who are you?" Leah asked. She'd asked him before and he hadn't given her an answer.

"Does that matter? Why don't I tell you my proposal?"

"I think you owe me your name. Otherwise I'll finish this coffee and go back to getting covered in fleas with Milly the Dachshund."

He just smiled, saying nothing.

"Is it a secret? Because if it is, that might scare me more than the stalking."

The smile grew smaller, he looked almost bashful. "It's Seth."

Leah turned the name over in her mind. What sort of name was it? Biblical. Did this strange scenario feel better now he had a label?

"I'm putting on a show. It's a new play, never been performed before. The female lead is a highly-privileged daughter of a high-ranking MP. To cut a long story short, she falls in love with the man sent to assassinate her father."

She scrunched up her face at the premise. "It sounds more like a book than a play."

"It will be one day. And a film. If it goes down well."

"And you're the director?"

Seth shook his head. "No, that's my father."

She didn't understand. This wasn't how you got auditions – meeting people in the street, them finding out where you work and buying coffee.

"I'm not selling this very well, am I?" Seth put his hands to his head and took a deep breath inwards. He was nervous, tingling with hot and cold pins and needles. At any minute he could break into a sweat. It was never attractive and he never had any control over it.

"You want me to audition for this part?" Leah guessed.

Again, Seth shook his head. "No. The part's yours, if you want it."

A bewildered expression was set on her face now, her eyes on him, her brow furrowed. He needed to just tell her. Tell her everything. She would feel sorry for his situation and she would agree straightaway. All he needed to do was tell her why he had to do this. He opened his mouth to speak.

"Why didn't you contact my agent?" she asked.

He didn't have an answer for that immediately, his mind was fizzing with scenarios if he said certain words, her reactions to them, what would happen.

"I wanted to meet you in person. I wanted to see the girl who brought Rosalind to life in *Lost & Alive*."

With those words it was like he'd flicked a switch. Across the table from him she seemed to awaken with the memory of that role. As he watched her he imagined her recalling the drama, the tragedy, the intensity. He was certain no one could play that part without feeling at least some of the character's pain and anguish.

"Sophia Hunt is a complex character, Leah. She's led this sheltered existence, protected by her father's status. Private school, monitored friends, money to burn on designer labels. Then her eyes are opened to her father's real life. The darkness of politics, the horror of war and love... love like she's never known."

The passion in his words were sending waves of shivers over her body. She had never heard anyone talk this way before. To strip themselves emotionally right before her. Because that's what he was doing. He was talking about something that touched the very depths of his soul. Something that moved him completely. Something he believed in. A fictitious story that rocked his balance, asked him questions in the real world.

His hand shook as he picked up his coffee cup and put it to his lips. She didn't know if she could speak yet. Her stomach was churning, her mind buzzing with a thousand questions but she didn't know which one was coming first. An amalgamation of fear and thrill was combining inside her.

"Where is this going to debut?"

Internally she cursed herself. That was the least important question of them all. She wanted to know more about the story – about the MP, his wife, Sophia's lover, how they all connected.

Seth put his cup down and shifted in his seat. "I'd need you to start rehearsals straightaway. I'm almost there with the cast, just a few minor things to sort out. Sets are being built, everything's on course

– more or less. But I need a leading lady."

He hadn't answered her question. Did it matter? Did she need to know where it was? She'd just experienced the same sensation she'd got from reading the first couple of pages of the script of *Lost & Alive*. And she hadn't read a word yet. Just heard one impassioned pitch that had re-ignited her desire to perform.

Seth put one hand over the other in a bid to stop them shaking. He could feel the perspiration forming on his body but he was desperate not to let it show. He had seen the way Leah had looked when he told her about the play. *His* play. The one thing he was going to get right, for his father, for the whole family and, more importantly, for everyone he had chosen. It was about the future, giving something back.

She opened her mouth, as if she was about to say something, but then she stopped, closed her lips again. She was still looking at him and he was hanging, suspended in space, waiting, wanting, needing to know the answer whichever way it went.

Leah opened her mouth and finally spoke. "I never accept a job without reading the script. How am I meant to know it's right for me?"

Seth swallowed, sensing the "no" to come. His whole insides were freefalling down to his shoes, the colour draining from his face. There wasn't time for her to read the script before her agreement and that wasn't how things had to be. Her performance, her reaction to the story, the words and direction had to be fresh for this to work the way he wanted it to. It was as much about the actors' movement to the tale as it was about the audience response.

"Leah, I'm not asking you this time. I'm begging you."

It was a plea. He let his hands go, let her see the shaking and the nerves, tried to communicate his passion through eye contact alone. He saw her swallow.

She didn't know what to do. The role sounded challenging, the story original and unique but she couldn't make a decision like this when she knew nothing about this man, nothing about the play, nothing about how it would all pan out.

But the way he was looking at her now was nothing short of frightening. His hands were shaking, there were tears in his eyes and she knew there was something else, something he wasn't telling her. He looked desperate.

He took a breath inwards and stabilised himself, gripping the table with his hands, before holding them up in surrender.

"Truth?" he asked.

She found herself nodding.

"Okay." He paused, looked away for a second, then back to her again. "The reason I can't give you time is because I... we... don't have time."

His voice was faltering as he spoke and her heart sped up in reaction to the emotion. Whatever he was going to tell her it was serious. She put her hands into her lap and twisted her fingers together.

"Have you heard of David Marques, the film director?"

"Yes, of course. He's about the most famous director there is. Him and Steven Spielberg."

Seth nodded, the corners of his mouth raised slightly in a smile. "He'd like that."

She didn't know what to say. She couldn't imagine what was coming next.

"He's my father." He stopped short, knocked his coffee cup and had to straighten it. "And he's... he's dying."

He watched her hand fly to her mouth, pressed flat against her face, her eyes wide, her eyebrows heading towards her hairline. He let a gush of air come from his mouth. He knew he shouldn't have said it but she had to know how important this was and the reason there was such an urgency.

"No one knows, Leah. I'm trusting you to keep it that way."

She was already nodding her head up and down in quick succession.

"I just want to make him proud before it's too late. I've pulled some strings. We have a theatre for one week in a week's time. I need you to commit to the project, learn the lines in one read through, then perform it twice a week for seven nights."

He swallowed. It was all out. As much as he was going to share.

She nodded. "I don't need to hear any more." She smiled. "I'll do it."

It wasn't just a theatre. It was Broadway. *Broadway*. Just thinking the word brought goosebumps out on her skin. That night she was going to be performing on the iconic stage in the Booth Theatre.

"Are you going to eat those pancakes?" Seth asked.

Leah drew her eyes away from the New York scene rolling by outside the diner and back to him. They'd barely been apart this last week. It was all about the play, making plans, adjustments, making sure everything was ready for opening night. It had been such a quick turnaround but it was exciting and exhilarating and she had remembered exactly what she loved most about acting.

She dug her fork into her maple syrup covered breakfast. "I wonder what my dad's having for breakfast."

"You said your neighbour was going to drop in every night and keep an eye on him."

Mavis Jones had been offering to help as long as Leah could remember. This time she had gone to her and actually asked. She knew her dad was perfectly capable of looking after himself but it was a comforter, a safety net for her to know someone was looking out for him while she was away.

She nodded at Seth. "I know. But I also know how much he'll hate her dropping in. And how can-tankerous he can be. She'll wish she hadn't accepted."

He reached across the table and took her hands in his. She readily looped her fingers around his. They were friends, almost closer than friends. He'd intro-duced her to the rest of the cast and then his family. David Marques had a terrible cough and seemed to drink a lot of whisky.

"I know you said he doesn't want anyone to know but, do you think if the cast knew about your father's illness…"

Before she had even finished her sentence, Seth was shaking his head. "No, Leah. He doesn't want anyone to know. He doesn't want anyone's pity and that's what it would be like."

"It wouldn't be pity."

Seth gritted his teeth. "Yes it would. And that's *all* it would be."

She put her fork down and picked up her coffee cup. "People would want to be there for him."

"People would make the whole show all about the fact he's dying. I don't want that. That's the whole point. The play is all about the play and its performers, not the man behind it. You really think the strength of the story, the beauty and horror of it, would get a mention in the press if they knew?"

He was getting worked up and he needed to calm down and lower his voice. "I don't want the illness getting the headlines." He sighed. "And neither does he."

He ran a hand through his hair and took a breath. It was tonight. They were so close to the beginning of something so special. He needed to try and hold his nerve.

"I understand," Leah said. "So, seeing as the performance is tonight, isn't it time I met my leading man?"

He'd been waiting for her to ask that question all week. He'd made her practice the lines with one of the guys from crew. When the time came, when she actually performed, he wanted all her responses to be in the moment. Pure.

"Is it someone famous? With your dad's connections he could get anyone, couldn't he?"

He smiled at her. "Were you hoping for Brad Pitt?"

Immediately she shook her head. "Oh no, he would be awful! I've never rated him as an actor."

He laughed loud and hard then. "Next time he comes for dinner I'll let him know."

"Well... when do I get to meet him?"

"About ten seconds before curtain up," Seth replied.

Her heart was fluttering with the kind of palpitations she hadn't experienced in years. The theatre was full, every single seat taken – it was real. She was standing in the wings on Broadway, about to give everything she had for this role. She couldn't be more nervous, but not for herself. This was all about a dying man. If his last wish was to have this play light up the New York theatre district then she was going to make sure she put every ounce of energy and talent she had to give.

"You okay?"

Seth's voice whispering in her ear only heightened the fear and nerves.

"No, I'm just about terrified."

He smiled and took hold of her hand. "Don't be." He squeezed her fingers in his then brought them to his lips.

The softness of the action sent a curling momentum through her body. Just a week ago she was the face of the five-a-day campaign, now she was about to make her debut in the US.

"Time to meet your leading man," Seth said as Leah was beckoned onto the stage before curtain up.

"Tell me," she hissed, stepping forward.

"I'm right here," Seth said, falling into step behind her.

"It's me. It's my job to kill your father."

"No."

"I was never going to tell you. If I'd told you, you would try to stop me."

"I'm going to try and stop you now."

"Are you?"

"Yes."

"Even when you know what he's done. Even though you know what he's capable of? He's a murderer."

"Like you?"

"I am not like him."

"No? You don't use a gun to speak for you? You don't have secrets? You've never used someone to get what you want?"

"I have not used you."

"I'm not stupid."

"I love you."

"How can you say this?"

"Because it's true."

"You love me so much you're going to murder my father?"

"No. You are."

The gasp from the audience momentarily

brought Leah out of the play and into the realisation she was acting a part. Right from the outset, performing with Seth had been nothing like anything she'd done before. He was raw, he'd ad-libbed on several occasions but she found she could read him, knew what to do to make it work, almost instinctively. She shook her head, got back into the head of Sophia as the audience waited for more.

"You're insane."

"Maybe to some. Not to you. You know this has to be done."

"All I know is I made a horrible mistake getting involved with you."

"If that were true you would be calling for that omnipresent bodyguard to come to your rescue. But the fact is, you don't want to be rescued, do you?"

Seth had felt nauseous since the interval and now he had the most horrendous headache. It was making him dizzy, disturbing his vision and distracting him from the scene. It was only a few minutes until the end. He had to make it through. It was stress. It had been a full on couple of weeks putting everything together, it was bound to take its toll.

Leah walked towards him, stood close. It wasn't in the script. He knew she was checking up on him, could see there was something wrong.

"Answer me. You don't want to be rescued, do you?"

He was breathing so heavily, looking at her, a feeling engulfed her. She wanted to hold him. She wanted to kiss him. Not as her character Sophia, as Leah. She put a hand to his cheek and held it there, her gaze locking with his.

"All I know is, I want this to stop. Everything. The fighting, the lies, all of it."

"And it can. It can, Sophia, if we make it happen."

Slowly, inch by inch, she brought his face down to hers and held it there, their noses touching, their lips just short of touching.

"I cannot kill my father and I cannot let you do it either."

"Then, how do we go on?"

She pressed her lips to his, kissing him with every part of her. This wasn't written, it was natural, an instinct taking over. She ran her hands through his hair, clasping them at the back of his head as she felt him responding to her. This wasn't theatre, this was life, fiction and reality merging together, mingling into something so vital it was a heady mix burning her from the inside.

Before she could get the imitation gun out from under the silk dressing gown she was wearing Seth was falling. And then she was torn, everything happening so quickly yet at the same time so slowly. She had a second to make a decision. As he collapsed she fired the weapon and then she caught him in her arms, dropping to the floor with him as the curtains closed around them.

He hit the boards of the stage but he felt nothing. He was flying, high on what had happened. Everything. He'd achieved everything. Everything he'd dreamed of, everything he'd planned so meticulously. He'd done it and more. Because there was Leah. It had taken all his strength to keep things platonic in this last week when they'd shared meals, shared their passion for plays, shared her hopes for the future. If anything was going to happen between them it had to come from her. Because he'd lied. Because he didn't want her to know. Because it would have changed things.

And now he knew. Now he really knew how she felt for him. How, in these moments, she had wanted to hold him, to kiss him, to feel him, not as Lyle, as Seth Marques.

"Seth, speak to me! Someone! Get some help over here!"

She was crying now, tears spilling from her eyes as the sound of a thousand people clapping their hands together filled the theatre. There would be no curtain call tonight.

"Leah," he whispered.

She clasped his hands in hers. "You lied to me, didn't you?"

Her anguish hit him harder than the shards of white-hot pain pummelling his brain.

"Your father isn't dying, is he? You are."

She sobbed, burying her face in his chest as she wept.

He closed his eyes then and tried to steady his breathing as other people ran onto the stage to help.

"Don't... go back to advertising," he whispered. "Promise me that."

Leah raised her head, the tears constant.

"If I have to come back... and haunt you like Jacob Marley, I will." Seth smiled.

"Don't go," she begged.

"I think... this was my final encore. And... it was the best."

At the funeral she found out who Seth really was. Only twenty-five, destined to follow in his father's footsteps with a love for drama and film. As much as he adored acting, his joy was writing and *The Foreigner* had been his baby since he wrote it after his diagnosis. He'd chosen not to write something with a message about his disease, but a script about love and loyalty, a piece that would move people and stay with them for a long time. It would stay with Leah, as would the memory of what he had done for her, what they had shared together, how deeply she had felt in such a short time. It wasn't fair that someone so young, so vibrant and with so much still to give, should be taken so early, so brutally, with such cruelty.

"You need to eat, Lea," Len said.

She'd been stirring the cottage pie on her plate and not a morsel had made it into her mouth. She couldn't stomach it.

"I didn't make it. Mavis Jones brought it in yesterday."

She nodded. She didn't trust herself to speak without breaking down.

"Sorry about your friend. Did you know him well?"

Her dad's question had her choking up. The tears were at her eyes already. She shook her head.

Len reached across the table and patted her hand. "He's free from pain now, Lea. Safe up there with the angels."

She nodded and wiped her nose with the sleeve of her blouse. She needed to be strong.

Len unfolded his copy of *The Sun* and picked up an envelope off of the table. He handed it over to Leah.

"Forgot to give you this earlier. Came yesterday."

She looked at the writing, then at the US stamps.

Leah,

I usually think positive but I'm pretty sure we're not going to make a full week on Broadway. The way I'm feeling now I'll be lucky to make opening night. But I'm going to give it everything I've got and everything the medical profession has too.

So, by the time you read this, I'm pretty sure I won't be around giving you stage direction. But don't think that lets you off the hook. No matter what happens with the play I want you to know that you can stir something in an audience like no one I've ever seen. That's a God given talent you just can't ignore. Don't waste any more days doing things for money. Do things for life. Laugh, love and tell your lazy arse dad he needs to buck his ideas up. It's your life, Leah and, as I've found out, you only get one shot.

I don't want you to think I didn't tell you because I didn't care. It was because I cared too much. I've been in love with you since I first saw you. I spent five years thinking you couldn't be the only person who could make me feel that way, only to realise I should have waited by the stage door that night and asked you out. You probably would have said no and I would definitely have stalked you anyway.

I don't know how to say goodbye here, I hope I get to say it to you in person. I hope I get to hold you in my arms before the end and have the balls to

tell you some of this, but if I don't, know that you were so special to me and that this past week has been the best time of my life.
Seth x
p.s. My dad's working on a hard-hitting piece set in the 1960s. I've already told him you're perfect for the female lead. I know you won't want any favours but please audition. For me!

The End

Mandy Baggot is an award-winning romantic fiction author, writing hot heroes and emotional reads. In 2012 she won the Innovation in Romantic Fiction award at the UK's Festival of Romance. Her self-published title *Strings Attached* was also short-listed for the Best Author Published Read award.

Also in 2012 she signed with American publishing house, Sapphire Star Publishing, who produced her novels *Taking Charge,* and romantic suspense *Security.*

In June 2013 she signed a two book deal with Harper Collins' digital first romance imprint, Harper Impulse.

She is a regular contributor to writing blogs and online emagazine, *Loveahappyending Lifestyle* www.loveahappyending.com

Mandy loves mashed potato, white wine, country music, World's Strongest Man, travel and handbags. She has appeared on ITV1's *Who Dares Sings* and auditioned for *The X Factor.*

Mandy is a member of the Romantic Novelists' Association and lives near Salisbury, Wiltshire, UK with her husband, two daughters, and cats Kravitz and Springsteen.

Website: www.mandybaggot.com
FB: www.facebook.com/mandybaggotauthor
Twitter: twitter.com/mandybaggot

MODERN BOYS
by Rosie Dean

"So what about it, then?" Jake asked, nervously flicking ash from his cigarette.

At the other end of the line, a sigh betrayed Matt's indecision.

Jake seized the moment. "They'll all be there, you know. All the old fans. It'll be a great night."

Quietly, Matt responded, "Okay."

Jake stubbed his cigarette out fiercely, as if applauding Matt's decision.

"Brilliant! I'll get on to the other guys and fix it all up then. Aw, Matt, this is going to be a great gig. You're gonna love it."

Switching off his mobile, Jake let out a hoot of triumph. The Modern Boys, his boys, back in action in their home town. The greatest band to issue from the Isle of Wight, and he'd discovered them. He'd moulded them, fitted them up for stardom and watched them soar. It wasn't down to him that they'd broken up. No. That was the pressure of being away from their roots. And as for Rick Madison – fine manager he turned out to be – coming in waving bits of paper that promised great contracts. He didn't care about them like Jake did.

"Let me take you forward," Madison had coaxed. "You saw what I did with Jet-Jet. I can do the same for you guys."

So that's what they'd done. Moved up to London and made it into the charts with "Ain't Gonna Happen". Their Isle of Wight fans had filled the ferries getting up to London to see them at the Hammersmith Palais. That was an achievement in itself;

most of the fans hadn't been further than the funfair on Southsea beach. And, just when they seemed poised to hit the big time, Madison's other band, Ice, had shot to number one with a hollow, grating rap record, and his interest in The Modern Boys evaporated.

Inevitably they'd gone their separate ways. Only Matt was still in the business. He'd stayed with Rick, scouting for talent and helping to manage new bands that came along.

Now, fifteen years since their first gig, Jake was getting them back together. A benefit gig for the island's new concert hall. Right across the island, theatre groups and musical societies were doing their bit. With a million pound hand-out from the Lottery Commission, the concert hall was in their sights. What an event. Jake felt so excited, he thrust his face towards the mirror.

"There, you clever bastard. You've done it! It's finally gonna happen!"

Aaron, of Island Graffix, sat with his feet on the desk, wondering how he could get more business, bored with printing hotel menus and designing low-budget websites. As for theatre posters – there was no creativity in those: "We want black on a fluorescent background, Aaron. And remember to make the date nice and big."

He let his phone ring several times, while he stared at the poster roughs on his desk: Boot Sale and BBQ. He rolled his eyes and reached for the phone.

"Island Graffix."

"Jake here, mate. I hope you're sitting down 'cos I've got some brilliant news for you."

Gus learned the news from his answerphone, as he hovered in the hallway, unzipping his waxed jacket and stepping out of his shoes and into his slippers.

Beep. "Gus! Jake here. Give us a call when you get in."

Beep. "Gus! It's Aaron. I've just had Jake on the blower. I can't believe it. The Modern Boys are coming back! Fancy a drink over at the Folly tonight?"

Gus chuckled and padded down the hallway over the plastic matting that protected the carpet. He took a chicken pie from the freezer and switched the oven on. Returning to the hallway, he stood in front of the oval gilt mirror and struck his air guitar three times. "Ain't Gonna Happen!" he sang and then grinned as he returned to the kitchen and scanned the shelves for a tin of beans.

Dave was harder to track down. Jake didn't know where Dave lived now and his parents were dead, so he went straight to the top – IBM head office. The operator was very polite.

"We have four Dave Smiths in IBM UK. Can you give me any more information?"

Jake drew deeply on his cigarette. "Tall, dark haired bloke. Comes from the Isle of Wight."

"Does he commute?"

Jake frowned. "Nah. He's a programmer."

The receptionist made a stifled noise. "I see. Let

me put you through to our Winchester office."

Dave was in the States for two weeks. His team leader, happy to pass on a message, was treated to a potted biography of The Modern Boys, until the call failed. Jake glanced at his phone – two bars. Oh well. At least he'd made contact.

It might be old and dusty but Jake's wagon was rolling again. He hadn't forgotten how. Within days he was onto Radio Solent for some PR.

"This is what I'm best at," he crowed before they went on air. Jan C Valentine, self-invented personality and radio presenter, nodded in agreement. Behind her dark glasses she examined a list of people she'd like on her show, and wondered if it might be worth trying for a lesser royal.

"You see, I knew how to motivate those boys, that's how we did so well."

"Mmm." Jan C scribbled *Pippa Middleton?* on her clipboard.

She beamed Jake a smile any observant dentist would recognise as being a pricey one. "Great, Jake. Great! Now, we're on air for twenty minutes before we bring you in. Help yourself to coffee." She wrinkled her nose in a gesture of forced friendliness as she stood up. "Okay?"

Jake watched her go, her backside wagging provocatively – each cheek wobbling from too many wine bar dinners and not enough exercise. There was a time when he might have made a play for her, he thought, nipping outside for a quick smoke.

The broadcast brought the occasion to public attention. On the back of it, he had the promise of some editorial in the *County Press*, slots on Southern Focus and even a small corner of the national music press.

He bought a new distressed leather jacket, twenty Havana cigars and, now feeling back in the heady world of international music, altered his watch to Greenwich Mean Time.

Two weeks before the event, Matt rang Jake and insisted on a rehearsal in London.

"Nah," drawled Jake. "You wanna get over here. Back to your roots."

"I haven't time to come over. We've got studios here we can rehearse in, for free, with all the best equipment."

"Matt, we want it like the old times," Jake wheedled. Then added more definitely, "I've already agreed it with Aaron. We can use Ventnor Cricket Club."

Matt stared at the calendar above his desk. Their top star had two nights at the Royal Albert Hall; a gold disk presentation at Virgin; dinner at the Groucho Club with a dozen other muso types… and rehearsals at Ventnor Cricket Club. He shook his head and laughed. Not the staccato laugh he used for Rick's weak attempts at humour, not the flirtatious laugh he saved for clients he negotiated deals with, but a genuine belly laugh. He wiped tears from his eyes.

"I'm sorry, mate. It'll have to be up here. There's just no way I can do it otherwise."

"But the press were gonna be there, Matt."

"Look, the press can come here if they like. But I

can't get over to the island before the gig, and that's it, mate."

"All right, all right," Jake submitted, rolling his cigarette backwards and forwards between his fingers. "Give me the address."

Aaron and Gus met at the wet end of Ryde pier to catch the catamaran. A cool, damp wind whipped around them, making their guitar cases unwieldy. Jake rushed towards them, his thinning hair stirred up like twitch grass. "Here we go, boys, here we go!"

Dave stood waiting for them on the other side, outside Portsmouth station, his drum-kit loaded into the back of his people carrier.

His old mates weren't difficult to recognise. Two thirty-something men with guitars and overnight bags were a dead give-away. Jake was still the same swaggering gut-bucket he'd always been, if a little greyer – both in hair and skin tone.

Greetings of "How ya bin?" and "All right, mate?" rang out, along with much shoulder slapping and chest punching – which confirmed that male bonding never dies, just gets more physical.

They piled into the MPV. "Makes a change from ten-year-olds with football kit," Dave said, apologetically wiping crisp crumbs from one of the seats.

A couple of miles into the journey, when conversation strayed from old world reminiscence into new world achievements, the chemistry between them became tangibly unstable. This noted, Dave switched on the DVD player. As they recognised the first chord, a cheer went up in the back.

"Ain't gonna happen" happened.

Matt stared out of the studio window onto the congestion in the street two floors below. There was noise, colour, activity – Matt had been hooked from the first moment he'd stepped onto the busy London streets. He'd nothing to go back to the island for now. Apart from his mother.

His eyes followed the snaking line of commuters making their way home. Further off, to the left, he saw a large, blue, people carrier, halfway across the junction. It inched forward and stopped abruptly. Cars ahead of it began making progress, cars behind it did not.

There was a hoot from an impatient driver. The MPV moved slightly to the right and stopped. Two more hoots of irritation rang out. A passenger in the blue vehicle came into view as he craned forward, scanning the buildings for clues. A cigarette smouldered between his lips.

"Oh God!" moaned Matt, before running down two flights of stairs and out into the street. For one terrifying moment, he thought the driver was contemplating a three-point-turn.

Gus felt his stomach tighten as Dave edged the space cruiser forward another few inches.

"I'm sure it's back that way. If this traffic cleared a bit we could turn round."

"What's that prat doing over there?" asked Dave, as Matt ran out from between two parked cars, waving frantically.

"Bloody-ell!" exclaimed Aaron. "It's the old crooner himself!"

While the band set up, Jake was like a kid at his own birthday party – rushing round and showing off.

"This is it, boys. This is the life." He couldn't stop himself from giving random impulsive hugs.

"So have you got the press coming, then?" asked Matt.

"Nah! Got a busy week." He screwed his eyes up as a draft blew smoke into his eyes. "Aaron's got a camera though, haven't you, mate?"

Once the talking was done, the rehearsal began.

Guitars twanged and growled.

"What's first, then?" Dave asked.

Matt and Jake began speaking together. Matt wanted to warm up on standard rhythm and blues, Jake preferred to take a shot at "Ain't Gonna Happen".

For a moment they all looked at one another, at the floor, at their instruments.

"Okay, let's try 'Ain't Gonna Happen'," Matt conceded, strumming three quick chords as he took up his stance by the mike.

It was a debacle. They all knew the notes, the tune and words but they'd forgotten how to bind them together.

Matt held his hand up to prevent further damage. "Come on, guys, we need to find the groove. Aaron, give us some bass."

After four bars he gave Dave a nod, then Gus on

rhythm and finally he picked up on lead. Cool grooving rhythm and blues.

Jake sat to the side, tapping his foot and nodding his head. He smiled to himself. "Now we're cookin' with gas."

"Welcome to Southern Focus. In tonight's programme, we bring you a story of the new donkey sanctuary that's causing a stir; Lisa visits a lady in Hedge End who's celebrating her one hundredth birthday, and I'll be looking into the mystery of the disappearing rudders. But first, over to Richard in the Isle of Wight, where history is being recreated as nineties band, The Modern Boys, re-form for a charity concert."

"Thanks, Kate. Yes, fifteen years ago this week The Modern Boys first performed a song that was to become a top twenty hit for them."

The screen faded to an amateur video, shot by Aaron's dad. The image was blurred and, wisely, had been re-dubbed with the professional recording. Halfway through the first chorus it faded back to Richard, who had been joined by Jake, complete with distressed leather jacket and cigar.

"Jake, you first discovered the band in a school concert, here in Cowes."

"That's right. Great moment."

"It must be quite nostalgic to have brought them back together again, on their home turf."

"Oh, yes. They were always a great band – still are. And when I approached them about doing this to raise money for the Isle of Wight Concert Hall, they were only too happy to help out."

"Giving a bit back, eh?"

"Absolutely. Music means everything to us – just like it does to thousands of kids out there."

"Two of The Modern Boys still live on the island, but one is actually in the music business."

"That's right. Matt Noble manages Ava and The Movement, among others."

"Any likelihood he might want to re-form The Modern Boys permanently, do you think?"

Jake smiled and nodded. "Well, Rich, you can never tell in this business."

"Yes you bloody can!" Matt chuntered, as he paused playback on the TV in his mother's flat.

Once his office had heard about the reunion, he'd had a full fortnight of ribbing from his colleagues and clients. Despite winding them up in return, he had absolutely no intention of re-forming the band permanently.

He was even questioning the wisdom of agreeing to do this gig.

His mobile rang. It was quarter past midnight. He snatched it up to avoid waking his mother.

"Matt? You're there!" Jake's voice sounded coarser than ever, the cigars and the interviews were taking their toll.

"You coming down the Night Owl?"

"No thanks, Jake. I've only just arrived."

"Come on, Matt. I've got Duke and Marti here. You remember, from the old Cleo's Club. The boys are all pestering me to get you over."

Matt looked at the carton of apple juice he'd been drinking and listened to the comforting hiss of the gas fire.

"Jake, I'm tired."

"Come on, it won't be the same without you. Just this once."

Matt sighed. He knew when he'd been emotionally cornered. "Where is it?"

"Down on the Esplanade, where Wild Bill's used to be."

Matt walked down the hill towards the seafront, and welcomed the blast of sea air on his tired head. Turning onto the Esplanade, the Night Owl came into view. He always avoided clubs in London. They were a part of the scene he didn't enjoy. The throb of a James Brown track oozed under the door. A stocky lad with a shaved head, six earrings and a dinner suit, asked if he had a membership card.

"No. Jake Fergusson's expecting me."

"Name?" the lad asked, perusing a small WH Smith notepad.

"Matt Noble."

"Thank you, Mr Noble." He pushed open the door. "Straight ahead, sir."

Matt stepped into the dimmed bar-cum-nightclub. Jake, the boys and their partners were seated in a group in the far corner. His eyes were immediately drawn to them – had to be – the rest of the club was empty. Empty save for the barman in a brightly coloured shirt and reading the *County Press*.

Saturday morning and Jake was out early. For the

first time in years he took a walk down to the beach and tossed some stones into the sea. The last couple of months had been a real tonic for him – almost a rebirth.

The postman arrived at Jake's gate at the same time as he arrived home.

"All right, Bob?"

"Morning, Jake." He handed him a letter. "There you go, recording contract from Virgin."

"I'm holdin' out for Universal, mate!" Jake grinned as he took the small brown envelope, tearing it open.

He wandered through his open front gate and read the letter, stuffing it into his pocket as his mobile rang.

It was Gus. "Guess what? My green Doc Martens still fit!"

Waiting behind the curtain, Matt felt all the agony and ecstasy of fifteen years ago. Through the heavy drapes they could hear the buzz of the crowd. He looked at Aaron, who stared in concentration at the stage. Dave sat beating a frantic rhythm in the air with his drumsticks. The intervening years concertinaed out of sight, leaving here-and-now juxtaposed with there-and-then.

Beyond the curtains, the lights went down. In response, the crowd hushed – apart from a few random cat-calls and whistles.

All became still.

Matt licked his lips.

The lights went up again.

The boys looked at one another.

"What the f—"

The crowd jeered.

The lights dropped again.

"Bloody amateurs!" Matt muttered through clenched teeth.

The curtains peeled back. Lights flooded the stage, and at Matt's signal, the band hit the first chord.

The crowd rose to its feet, the roar drowning the first few bars. In the wings, Jake's blood seemed to fizz through his veins like dandelion and burdock.

"This is it, ya clever bastard!" he said "This is it!"

An hour and three encores later, The Modern Boys jostled around backstage, slapping backs, hugging friends and punching chests. They shook with hysterical laughter.

Jake was euphoric. "Brilliant. Absolutely fuckin' brilliant! You boys are the best. I love the lot of ya!"

Matt stood, his eyes glistening with a forgotten joy. "Jake!" he said, throwing his arm around his shoulder. "Jake, thanks a million, mate. I wouldn't have missed this for the world."

The others joined in a group hug.

"Holy crap," exclaimed Dave. "We should do this again in another ten years!"

"Ten years?" shouted Aaron. "We wanna get a gig at the new concert hall when it opens next year. Waddya say?"

"Next year!" they cheered, holding their cans aloft. "Next year!"

Half an hour later, Jake sucked hard on a cigar as he watched Dave load the last of his kit into the MPV. He thought about the letter in his pocket: Please arrive at the Chemotherapy Unit at 09:15 and be prepared to stay for most of the day…

"Same time next year, eh, Jake?" Dave grinned at him and climbed into the driving seat.

Jake gave him the thumbs up as the van's engine spluttered into life.

He looked around – the weight of nostalgia in his heart.

There was nothing more to do here. It was time to go home.

The End

Rosie Dean: "I write romantic fiction with a sense of humour and, sometimes, a sense of the ridiculous. Because we all know life and love aren't exactly how we'd like them to be.

When not writing, I love to cook and to read, I even read in the car (talking books) and have notched up countless unnecessary miles as a result.

Not one to spend hours in the gym or pounding the pavement, I prefer Yoga and Pilates, which means I can tone and tighten whilst watching TV."

Rosie's works include: Women's Contemporary Fiction – Romantic Comedies *Millie's Game Plan (Nov 2013)* and *Vicki's Work of Heart (Mar 2014)*. Short story: *Captivating Sacha,* included in Harlequin, Mills & Boon anthology, *Truly, Madly, Deeply* (E-version) and *Truly, Madly, Deeply Part 9* (E-version).

Website: www.rosie-dean.com
Email: rosiedean.author@gmail.com
Twitter: twitter.com/RosieDeanAuthor

SACRIFICE
by **Linn B Halton**

"I'm sorry, Ashleigh." Sean's body slumps as he begins speaking. "I can't do this any more. You deserve someone who can offer you a long-term commitment. You deserve better than *this*."

The love of my life toys with his starter, as I look at him in a state of total shock and disbelief. What? My thoughts are screaming *retract the question*, unable to comprehend this sudden turn in the conversation. All I asked was whether he was free to go on a jolly the weekend after next. My boss is rewarding me for services rendered with a luxury weekend away for two. Well, landing a huge contract to supply surveillance equipment to a chain of night clubs, to be precise. I thought Sean would be thrilled at the thought of our first weekend away together after nearly six months of dating. I'm aghast by his response.

We're over? What did I miss? I thought everything was going really well, albeit we both have busy careers and only get to see each other a few times each week. I try to keep my breathing steady, although my heart is thumping so loudly in my chest that I wonder if he can actually hear it. My eyes are threatening to fill with tears and, in an attempt to stave them off, I curl each hand up into a tight ball in my lap. As my fingernails bite into my palms, I focus on the physical pain in an attempt to detract from the emotional one. Casting a glance around the restaurant, I wish we were somewhere private; somewhere it was easier to talk.

"Um... it was only a thought, if you can't make

it…" My voice is uneven as I desperately attempt to recover the situation. I'm trying really hard to sound, if anything, blasé. If he really has changed his mind about our relationship, then I need to find out why, because this feels like a random lightning bolt. There must be something I can do, this can't be *it* as in *we're over*, can it?

As I try to clear my thoughts, I find myself involuntarily shaking my head in sheer disbelief. Fortunately, Sean doesn't lift his eyes to meet mine, as his fork continues to rearrange the salad on the plate in front of him. His body language, though, is crystal clear. It's the first time I've ever seen him like this – so dejected, I want to rush up from my chair and hug him.

"I should've said something before. I feel really bad about it. I wasn't trying to mislead you, Ash-leigh, but I think it's for the best."

I gulp back the tears, relieved that he's still too embarrassed to raise his head to look directly at me. *What shall I do? What shall I do?* I'm in love with you, damn it! You sucked me in with your charm and Mr. Nice Guy image. Am I that bad a judge of character that I couldn't see your heart wasn't in it, while I was so stupidly opening mine up to you? Am I destined to pick the wrong man for the second time? Okay, you haven't cheated on me… then it hits me. Maybe that's already happened and the guilt is now too much for him to bear. A whole weekend away together – forty-eight blissful hours, or so I thought – is maybe too long a period to keep up a charade. I was dreaming of waking up next to you and you were occupied with how on earth you were going to wriggle out of *us*.

I wipe my mouth with my napkin, place it gently down next to the plate, and push my chair back noisily. Drawing in one long, deep breath for courage, I stand and gaze down at him as dispassionately as I can. That's not easy to do when you are madly in love with someone, even if they have just ripped your heart out of your chest.

"It was nice knowing you," I whisper. I turn and walk out of the restaurant with my head held high, trying to look cool and in control. The minute the chilly evening air hits me I almost collapse, only my inherent stubbornness keeps my legs going.

"He said *what*?" Lisa looks almost as shocked as I felt when Sean delivered the blow.

"He said he hadn't been trying to mislead me and I deserved better."

My fingers fold the empty sugar wrapper in half, then half again as if I'm an expert in origami.

"Stop fiddling, you need to rewind – what did I miss?"

At least I now have the tears under control, but it's still difficult to talk about it. I keep going over and over it in my head, torturing myself about the clues that would have been there, but which my subconscious obviously chose to ignore.

"I know, I feel the same way," I admit, trying very hard not to sound as if it isn't the end of my world. It is, of course, and everything seemed to fold in on me over the weekend. I felt as if I was trapped in a little bubble of misery. The first time in a long while that I trust someone enough to let go of my insecurities, and let them see the real *me*, this happens.

"I don't believe it," Lisa exclaims. "My gut instincts can't be that wildly off-mark. I always thought he was a little…"

I wrench my head upwards, almost too scared to gauge her expression. What? A little… what? Did she sense something I failed to see that had been there from the start? Did Sean have a commitment problem? He's thirty-two and claimed to have only one previous, meaningful relationship. When we had that awkward *let's share our past* conversation, I felt that it was something we actually had in common. How laughable! I assumed, because he didn't go into detail and the fact that I'd just told him that my ex, Joe, had cheated on me, that he'd had been through the exact same thing. It's what he'd implied, and at the time I remember thinking it established another common bond between us. Goodness, if that wasn't the case and he'd been lying, then he probably thought what a loser I was, unable to keep my man from straying. I focus on Lisa, fearing what she's going to say.

"…wounded." There's the same level of empathy reflected in her tone that I'd felt.

"Nice guy, honourable intentions. Same here, but he didn't make any attempt to explain why it was suddenly all over between us. He sat opposite me unable to make eye contact and he didn't move a muscle to stop me when I walked away from him."

"And there's been no contact, since?"

"Nothing, total silence. Like it never happened, you know, us." I have to stop myself there. The tears are beginning to creep up on me again and my eyes are stinging. It takes a huge amount of effort not to dissolve into a sobbing heap. I have to take a few deep breaths before continuing.

"I thought we were perfect for each other. I remember admitting to him that it was a relief we'd been through the same thing. People of our age have all sorts of baggage and some of it is harder to handle than the rest. He seemed to understand the pain of having opened up your heart to someone, only to end up feeling betrayed and isolated. I thought we were both on the same page, metaphorically speaking. I was desolate after finding out I'd been cheated on the first time around, but now I feel like my life really is over. My heart is too broken to ever mend again."

Lisa extends her hand and gently covers mine, giving it a sisterly squeeze.

"It doesn't make any sense, Ash, and I'm not just saying that simply to make you feel better. That night I met Sean for the first time, I watched his eyes light up whenever he looked at you. He was in love and it was obvious. He wasn't making any attempt to hide it. There is no way anyone could keep up that sort of pretence for a whole evening under my scrutiny. That would be worthy of a practiced conman. My guy-dar would have sussed him out, believe me, I've met a rat or two."

"I guess I simply have to move on and accept what's happened."

Maybe I'm destined to be alone forever. What choice do I have? You can't make someone love you, can you?

Sliding into bed at nine thirty, I pick up my Kindle and search through the library for some light reading. Finding something that doesn't have any connection whatsoever to romance is harder than I thought. After searching through five screens, the only book I spot is one entitled *Eating, Emotions and Making Choices*. I came across it on Amazon shortly after my split with Joe, two years and four months ago. I remember thinking that it might come in handy, fearing I would spiral downwards into the black abyss of comfort eating. The fact that now is the first time I've felt the need to dip into it, reflects how much Sean meant to me. I didn't really know what love was until I met him, I just thought I did. With Joe it began with lust. It quickly declined into an awkward sort of friendship between two people who, it turned out, didn't have very much in common. Another thing I didn't realise until I had the benefit of hindsight.

Since walking away from Sean, I now know what true heartache is and how devastatingly empty life can feel without hope. He was special – kind, thoughtful and loving, or so I thought. Maybe a bit too loving, as it turns out, and I wonder who else he was getting cosy with on the evenings and weekends he was *away working*?

At least my job allows me to switch off from my emotions, as I'm crazily busy at the moment and there's no room inside my head to think, or feel, while I'm there. I've become a robot, pushing away anything remotely personal because I have no choice. I wake up each morning as if nothing has changed, still frantically trying to come to terms with this monstrous void inside of me. If it weren't for the fact that clearly my heart is still functioning, I'd argue that Sean had burst it like a balloon. It lay in my chest, empty and deflated. However, sleep is virtually impossible, so I need something to read that won't have anything in it to remind me that, yet again, I'm alone and loveless.

I glance down at my Kindle. Chapter one: "Can You Trust Yourself?" Here goes, I'm hoping this will have the same effect as counting sheep.

The next time I look up, the clock is telling me it's one thirty in the morning. My goodness, this book is thought-provoking. I check the blurb at the back and see that the author is Dr Sally Osborn, who is a motivational speaker. Her own life has been a constant battle with emotional problems and ill health. If my eyes weren't so heavy, I'd keep reading but another four hours and it will be time to get up again.

I wake up just before the alarm is due to go off. My mind is trying to make sense of a dream that feels like it was a challenge, if only I could remember it in full. No doubt inspired by my night time reading material, but work and Sean were all in there somewhere. What will happen if I can't let go of him? What if I never move on past this phase and become unable to feel, or trust someone, ever again?

That thought doesn't leave me all day, until eventually I arrive home and admit defeat. Something in that book has sown a seed in my head; it's wrong, but I can't ignore it. In desperation I decide to ring Lisa, hoping she won't try to talk me out of my little plan.

"Lisa, can I run something past you?"

"Hey, Ash, of course, fire away."

I'm not sure where to start, so I tell her a little about the book I'm reading.

She's impressed. "It sounds fascinating. Maybe I should read it, too."

"You should, but it's given me an idea. I'm not sure you'll approve and it's probably illegal, but I need your help." Several seconds of silence elapse. "Are you still there?"

"Yes, Ash, I'm here. Taking drugs isn't the answer, lovely; you will get over this …"

"Drugs? No, I didn't say an illegal *substance*; it's more of an illegal act. Dr Sally Osborn says that people often kid themselves they are coping and can't admit they are comfort eating. She suggests installing a small camera in the kitchen. You can link it to your laptop, or pc, and the camera never lies. I'm going to talk to one of our installation engineers, after all, I work with people who are industry experts when it comes to surveillance equipment."

"Ash, I saw you just over a week ago. You might have been on a chocolate binge, or something, in the meantime but it's way too early to say you have issues with food. I'm sure this doctor is talking about people who have a long-term problem. Weight gain that is causing them serious health…" She sounds anxious. I immediately jump in to reassure her.

"No. This isn't to monitor my trips to the kitchen, but to find out the truth. Maybe then I can accept what's happened. If Sean is involved with someone else, as sad as it sounds, I need to see that for myself. I still can't believe his feelings for me have changed. It doesn't seem real and I wake up each morning thinking he's still a part of my life. I'm hoping it will make my heart do a three hundred and sixty degree flip. I simply can't turn love into hate unless I have an indisputable reason to stop caring for him."

"Have you lost your mind? Breaking and entering into someone else's home is a criminal offence." Lisa's voice recoils in horror.

"Not inside his house, I was thinking more of inside a car parked opposite his house. I need to swap cars with you, as Sean has no idea what you drive." I hear a sharp intake of breath and then a few moments elapse as she slowly exhales.

"Could I be arrested for aiding and abetting a crime just by listening to you? Oh, Ashleigh – I know how bitterly disappointed you are, but this smacks of desperation! Is this really what it will take to get your life back on track?" She sighs, and I feel even guiltier than I did at the start of the conversation.

"Yes," I reply, meekly, feeling more than a little ashamed of myself.

"Then the answer is an uncomfortable *yes*, but I can only hope and pray we won't get caught out. The moment you can see for yourself what's going on, you have to promise me you will accept the inevitable. That first flush of love is amazing, but when things settle down that's the real test of whether a relationship has staying power. I have no doubt at all we didn't misjudge him, Ash. Obviously his feelings changed and at least he had the decency to understand you would be devastated.

It was brave of him to face up to it, rather than let it continue under false pretences. If you begin stalking him, though, I'll ring the police myself. I know you are hurting and you need answers, but I'm not going to stand back and watch my sister turning into some crazed woman out for revenge."

"Understood, and I promise. If he's with another woman, then I know that I can't blame him if his feelings for me changed for a genuine reason. One thing the book has encouraged me to do is to look at the situation with Joe in another light. I no longer feel like a victim because I can now see that I was just as much to blame as he was. We both chose to ignore the warning signs that we were growing further and further apart. Neither one loved the other enough to fix the problems. But with Sean, it's different. And the book also says that sometimes you have to take a risk and lay bare…"

"Enough! You've convinced me and I'm going to have to read this book that has you so fired up!"

"You're one in a million, sis."

I spoke to Matt at work, he owed me a favour and, besides, I was convinced it wasn't really illegal. Immoral maybe, and an invasion of a person's privacy, but that's what love does for you. It turns you into a desperate soul who will go to any length to get slapped in the face. I'm being facetious here, of course. I didn't feel I was implicating Matt in any way as I didn't tell him the whole story. Matt is simply installing a standard car CCTV security system into my sister's car. I purchased it, on his recommendation, from the Internet and he did something clever to enhance the range of the camera for the fun of it. Techie people are like that, they enjoy a challenge.

"It's independently battery operated and this is the best kit available on the market today," he'd informed me.

It was all coming together so perfectly when he dropped the bombshell. "Of course, it's only legal on private property. You can't point it at a public pathway, or the highway, because that infringes the rights of the general public."

It sounded like one infringement too far…

But I *have* to know the truth and the only other option is to sit in the car and keep watch. When I admitted to Lisa that Matt had worried me about breaking the law, surprisingly, instead of throwing up her hands in horror and backing out, she was prosaic.

"Twenty-four hours, no more. We take it in turns to do four-hour shifts. Then you walk away, whether you have the answer you're looking for, or not. Deal?"

Sitting in the car outside of Sean's house feels wrong. Lisa is right and I feel like a stalker. Sean has a right to his privacy and the longer I sit here, the more I find myself hoping he's away on business for a few days and nothing happens. I've been sitting here since six o'clock this morning and the only person to approach his terraced, three-storey Victorian house, was the postman. I felt sorry for him, as each of the houses has a stone staircase leading up to the front door. Aesthetically it looks quite grand, but it must be hard on the knees. Fifteen steps in all and it's a long road with at least seven ranks of houses.

The street begins to get busy around seven thirty, when the world en masse seems to wake up and people head out to work. Then it's the kids being ferried to school in cars, or walking in groups along the road, laughing and joking as kids do. There's no sign of any movement at all in Sean's house. Lisa arrives at ten o'clock for the first changeover. She slides into the passenger seat.

"What's happening?" she asks, and I find myself staring at her in disbelief. She's wearing a wig and a hideous beige raincoat I can't recall ever having seen her wearing before.

"Um... well... nothing. No movement whatsoever. I'm not even sure he's at home."

Lisa's face reflects disappointment; was she hoping that it would all be done and dusted by now and I'd have my answer?

"You haven't changed your mind?" I have to ask the question because if she says yes, then it will give me the excuse I need to call it all off.

I think she's frowning, but her forehead is totally hidden beneath the most ghastly fringe I've ever seen in my life. There's no movement in it whatsoever and the harsh line of the cut almost totally obscures her eyebrows, too. For a disguise I suppose it works, but it makes her look distinctly odd. It's hard not to laugh, but that would be mean.

"No, I gave you my word and I'll stick to it. Make sure you're back promptly at two o'clock. Is the camera on?"

"I decided it was best if we only turn it on if

something happens. If he's away then, technically, sitting in a car and keeping watch isn't breaking the law. If Sean is in there and decides to leave the house but he's on his own, then don't even bother flicking the switch."

"You sound like you've already given up." Lisa's eyes show the compassion she's feeling – even if the words are coming out of the mouth of someone who looks more like a stranger, than my sister.

"There's no point trying to love a man who doesn't love you back, is there? My head knows that, my heart can't quite accept it at this moment in time." I swing open the driver's door and Lisa climbs out of the passenger seat to walk around the car. She settles herself into the driving seat.

"Nice raincoat, Lisa," I remark, casually.

"I'm incognito," she retorts with a grin. "No one takes any notice of a person who wears beige." I find myself chuckling as I walk away from the car and head in the direction of the shopping area. Well, she certainly doesn't look like herself, but she's succeeded in looking like a woman you might want to cross the road to avoid.

It's an affluent area and the local shops reflect that. There's an interesting delicatessen, a Starbucks and a rank of shops displaying some rather expensive goods. There's everything from jewellery to shoes, as well as a small art gallery. However, it takes less than an hour to browse around each and every one of them. I'm not a natural window shopper, so it doesn't come easily to me to look as if I'm enjoying myself. Sales assistants seem to home in on me, wanting to engage me in conversation and tempt me with an impulse buy. Do I look gullible, I wonder?

Checking my watch, I realise I have no choice but to find myself a cosy little seat in Starbucks and hope they don't notice how long I stay. I doubt I can hang out there for the whole three hours remaining until I start my second watch. If I can while away an hour or two, then I could always take a walk back through the park opposite Sean's house. I should have jumped on a bus and returned home for a couple of hours. I hadn't thought this through properly and four hours is a long time to hang around without looking decidedly dodgy. I feel anything but casual, and as I walk through the door of the cafe I notice that the only free seat is in the window. Great, just what I needed.

Still, the coffee smells tantalising, and I order a croissant despite the fact that I'm not at all hungry. I figure that at least buys me the right to sit in here reading for a while, on the pretext that I'm passing time waiting for someone.

Manoeuvring around the tables to get to the empty chair isn't easy. It has been literally pushed back up against the wall in the far corner of the window. The table in front of it is tiny and that's why no one has chosen to sit there. Negotiating a double baby buggy, several handbags and a gap only the thinnest of super models could slide through, it's a relief to finally sit down. Attracting attention isn't exactly conducive to keeping a low profile and at least half a dozen people stare up at me as I tackle the obstacle course. A quick glance around now confirms no one is eyeing me suspiciously. I tug the Kindle out of my handbag and open it up with a sense of relief. I'm two-thirds of the way through Dr Sally Osborn's book and I know that it will quickly absorb me.

Chapter sixteen is amazing. In between sips of coffee and a few enforced mouthfuls of croissant, I feel her words are reaching out to me personally. When I'd initially picked up this book I had assumed from the title that it was going to be solely about eating habits in relation to negative emotions. However, it goes much further than that. This chapter is entitled "Suffering is Bittersweet"…

"We all like to suffer, don't we? It makes us feel worthy of those negative thoughts running around inside our heads. Everyone else you know is good at managing their lives and their relationships; obviously you are the odd one out. Well, the shocking news is that it isn't true. The reason you feel that way is because the only head you get to look inside is your own. There's almost a sense of arrogance in believing you are the only person in the world who is insecure, unable to make the right decisions and to whom bad things happen. I'm afraid the truth is that you are not alone."

Her words stop me mid-swallow and I end up in a coughing fit, as a piece of croissant lodges in my throat and refuses to move on down. I glance up, rather red-faced, and a few heads turn my way. The last thing I need now is for someone to have to perform the Heimlich manoeuvre on me. So much for keeping a low profile, in case Operation Sean goes wrong! It takes me a moment and several large gulps of coffee to regain my composure before I can return to my book. Wow, she's good.

"The need to suffer is like a drug. You can become hooked on it in much the same way as you can to cigarettes, alcohol, or pills. And now for another of my pet theories. If you are addicted to suffering, then you will be able to track that back to one major incident in your life. You know the one I mean. It was the moment you decided that you deserved whatever it was that happened to you. The danger with this particular drug is that it is self-perpetuating. Well, I'm here to bust your little bubble of righteous despair. In fact, what I'm going to give you, my friend, is some tough love. Addiction isn't healthy and if you choose it as a companion then your life is going nowhere. The choice is yours."

I raise my head up from my book feeling as if I've suddenly had my eyes opened for me. That's exactly what I'm doing to myself, isn't it? I'm feeding my own addiction. As I look around I can see that quite a few tables are now empty, like my coffee cup and it's probably time I ordered another. As I wait for my grande skinny vanilla latte with an extra shot, I consider Dr Sally's words. The truth is appalling. I need to see Sean with my replacement because that would allow me to wallow in the fact that yet another man has broken my heart. I don't know that he has done anything wrong and a relationship that is only six months old is still a young one. It's not as if we were planning to get engaged, or move in together. He hadn't made me any promises, or said anything to mislead me in any way. Sean is a nice guy and the fact that I ended up loving him more than he loved me, isn't his fault. But it hurt like hell and I seriously needed to hate him, because something deep inside of me wouldn't allow me to stop thinking about *us*. I guess it's time for me to say goodbye to my addiction.

"Can you make that to go, please?"

My sister is right, I have to move on whether I like it or not. Any suffering here is down to sheer stubbornness, because I desperately wanted Sean to be *the one*. Maybe Mr. Right was actually Mr. Wrong and all I need to understand is the *why*. Tough love indeed, Dr Sally, but knowing that the only person who can do anything about this is me, helps. It also puts *me* back in control.

The moment I open the passenger's door Lisa looks up at me with a distinctly fraught look on her face.

"What's wrong?" I pass her the Starbucks cup, disappointed that I can't immediately launch into the little speech I'd prepared on my way back. The one suggesting we call it all off and she drives me home.

"Sean's in there. A woman knocked on the door about an hour ago. I fiddled with the camera, but managed to miss catching her as it was merely seconds before the door closed. It was the same when she came out about half an hour later, I should have left the camera switched on, or something. Sorry, Ash, I guess I'm not much good at this."

"It's okay. I've taken a long, hard look at myself and decided this is utterly ridiculous. It's time to go home."

Lisa stares at me, her jaw hanging loose and her

eyes flashing back and forth in a weird fashion.

"I'm sorry for dragging you into this, it was very wrong of me," I admit, sadly.

"It's too late for that!" Lisa hisses.

As I turn my head to see what it is she's looking at over my shoulder, I see Sean striding towards the car.

Lisa, Sean and I sit around the table in his kitchen in an uncomfortable silence. Lisa keeps trying to catch my eye, but I'm faking an interest in the Victorian reproduction wallpaper on the feature wall. It's a whole minute since I stole a glance at Sean, who was sitting back in his chair looking perplexed.

"Is someone going to say something?" His voice is bordering on angry. Out of the side of my eye I can see that Lisa is shifting around in her chair. Well, squirming would be a better description. I guess I have to...

"Daddee, can I have a drink please?" A voice filters down into the kitchen from one of the rooms above.

I glance across the table at Lisa. Her eyes are almost as big as mine, as we stare at each other in disbelief and then turn to face Sean. He lifts himself out of his chair, grabs a pink Disney cup from the cupboard and fills it with apple juice from the fridge. Grabbing a straw from another cupboard, he leaves the room without explanation.

"What on earth?" I whisper to Lisa, who looks aghast. "What exactly happened earlier on?"

"He let in the woman, who was probably in her early thirties. She was on her own though; there wasn't any sign of a child. The visit lasted about half an hour and he gave her a peck on the cheek when she left. I'd describe her as smart, wearing a business suit, very professional looking, but that's all I noticed."

The sound of Sean returning inhibits any further conversation. He enters the room and sits back down in his chair without saying a word.

"Sean, I... um... owe you an apology." Reluctantly I have to make eye contact with him, although what I feel like doing is leaping up from the chair and running out of the house.

With the decision to move on still fresh in my mind, I don't want to know the truth any more. It no longer matters, so I need to get Lisa and myself out of here as quickly as I can.

"I won't lie about this, but I can assure you I'm over it now. I wish this morning hadn't happened and I'm sorry for invading your privacy. Lisa was an unwilling accomplice and her motivation was one of sisterly love. Whatever I was hoping to achieve is now irrelevant, and I feel very foolish indeed. We'll leave you in peace."

I stand up and make an eye gesture at Lisa, so she's in no doubt that we need to make a quick escape. As she follows me into the hallway Sean's voice breaks the silence.

"Sit down, Ashleigh. You too, Lisa." We shoot each other a glance and Lisa's face seems to be implying we should ignore Sean and keep going. The front door is only a dozen paces away. "Please," he adds and his voice sounds hollow.

Lisa's look is one of frustration as I turn around and head back into the kitchen. She follows, rather reluctantly.

"I owe you an explanation and it's long overdue. Can I ask you one question first?"

I nod. He doesn't sound angry, but apologetic. I scan his face and his expression surprises me. He seems upset.

"Were you watching me, or have you been shopping and simply happened to park opposite my house?"

The temptation to lie is huge. I glance at Lisa, who is now so embarrassed by the whole situation she's staring down, rather miserably, into her lap.

"I've been sitting outside your house since six o'clock this morning." There's no point in making this any worse than it already is by spinning a fabricated story. I respect Sean too much not to be honest with him.

"Really? Why?"

That's the bit I don't want to answer, so I ignore his question and instead I meet his eyes with my own. We used to be so good at reading each other without words and with Lisa sitting here wishing the ground would swallow her up, there are things better left unsaid.

"It's all my fault." He expels the words with force. His face contorts with emotion and I wonder if he's going to… cry. I'm shocked beyond belief at his reaction and so is Lisa, whose head turns towards Sean, a mortified look plastered all over it.

"No, no. It's not your fault, Sean. You were honest with me and I, stupidly, refused to let go. I needed to see you with someone else to stop…" My words fade away; I can't say the "L" word now. I feel pathetic enough admitting to what happened

114

today.

"Ashleigh, please listen to me. I fell in love with you on our first date. The way you were so nervous you couldn't stop chattering away, I was flattered and I knew you were special. But some of the things you said hit home. When you told me how relieved you were that we both had a relationship history that wasn't complicated, an alarm went off in my head. Quite rightly, you pointed out how ex-spouses, and kids, could make it hard to move forward. I'm ashamed to admit I didn't tell you the whole truth."

I spin my head back to look at Lisa, who looks as shocked as I feel. He's going to tell me he's a married man, but his wife doesn't understand him... Dr Sally, you were wrong. Sometimes people suffer for a reason and that's because sometimes we're misled.

"Just listen, please. After you told me briefly about Joe, I left you with the impression the break-up of my relationship was under similar circumstances. It wasn't, and I know not telling you everything amounts to a lie."

"I'd rather not know the details, Sean. It's water under the bridge now. I'll forgive you that, if you forgive me for this morning's shocking little episode." The last thing I need now is the truth. I simply want to go home, curl up in bed like Sleeping Beauty and wake up at some distant point in the future when my feelings have shut down.

"I'm divorced and I have a six-year-old daughter. So yes, I have the ex-partner who is always going to be in my life demanding attention, even though what we had fizzled out a long time ago. And yes, because I share parental responsibility for my daughter it means half of each week I have someone else to put first. I was putting her before you, all the time we were seeing each other. I knew it was a lie I couldn't keep from you forever. I was hoping that when the time was right and I admitted it to you, our relationship would be solid enough to deal with it."

Lisa and I look at each other, totally shocked by Sean's outpouring. A few moments elapse while his words sink in.

"What changed?"

"Loving someone means wanting what's best for *them*. You deserve to have your dream with someone who not only loves you, but who doesn't have a life full of complications. A man who can give you his undivided attention, and with whom you can build a bright, new future. You deserve more than I can give you, Ashleigh. So I had to let you go. I'm sorry for the deceit and the pain I've caused you."

He stands, pushing his chair back from the table abruptly. His face reflects the pain attached to his words and my heart melts with a mixture of joy, sadness and pride in the man I love.

I glance at Lisa and her hands fly up to her cheeks, a look of disbelief reflected in her expression.

I'm on my feet and within mere seconds I'm in Sean's arms. My face is wet with tears and I don't think they're mine alone.

"You idiot," I murmur, half laughing, half crying. "Loving someone changes everything, but you don't know that until you meet *the one*. You are my *one* and I love you, baggage and all. Whatever matters to you, matters to me, too."

"Well, the little parcel I have upstairs is called Ruby and she has a sprained ankle at the moment. That's why her mother called around to see her this morning. We decided she's better off staying here for the first couple of days as she's happy enough watching DVDs. But, Ashleigh, it's a lot to ask of anyone to accept…"

I shush him then, snuggling into his body as a wave of happiness and relief floods through me. Dr Sally was right; sometimes you have to lay yourself bare and see what happens. My gut instinct had been telling me to hang in there, hoping for a miracle, something that would make everything right. Sean had been prepared to make the ultimate sacrifice because of those stupid words I'd spoken, without so much as a thought. It was nervous babble; that was all. Yes, his situation might have put me off a little on that very first date but I, too, had felt that instant connection. I wouldn't have run away, as he seemed to think. I would have taken it one day at a time, hopeful that if we did have something special, we'd find a way of coping with whatever came our way.

I glance at Lisa, whose eyes are full of tears.

"I think he's a keeper." I laugh, and she steps forward to throw her arms around us both.

I guess the sacrifices we make for those closest to our hearts speaks more about the love we feel than simply saying the words "I love you".

The End

Linn B Halton lives in the small village of Lydbrook, Gloucestershire in the UK, but was born in Bristol. She resides there with her husband and cat with "catitude" – Mr Tiggs.

"My stories are about love, life and real relationships – but romance is always the one thing that holds each story together. Often there's a light, psychic touch and I never dreamed I would write drawing upon my personal psychic experiences. But as my interest and understanding has grown in the subject, it is now such a part of my life it finds its way into my fictional tales. I hope it will make readers stop and wonder 'What if?'"

Love, life and beyond… but it's ALWAYS about the romance!

Linn is published by Harper Impulse and Sapphire Star Publishing. She won the 2013 Innovation in Romantic Fiction (Author Award) and her 2014 release, *Sweet Occasions*, was short-listed for the UK Romantic Fiction Author Published Award. She is also the editor-in-chief at *Loveahappyending Lifestyle* emagazine:

www.loveahappyending.com
Website: linnbhalton.co.uk
FB: www.facebook.com/authorlinnbhalton
Twitter: twitter.com/LinnBHalton

WHERE ANGELS FEAR TO TREAD
by Jenny Harper

Clemmie da Silva watched the red lights on the illuminated floor indicator as the lift sped upwards. Seven… eight… nine.

The lift floated soundlessly to a halt, the doors opened and a woman stepped in, her arms full of files.

"Press eleven for me, will you?" she asked, her voice heavily accented. Polish? Croatian? "I have no hands."

Clemmie leant over obediently and pushed the bright stainless steel button with the black number 11 on it. The lift doors slid shut with a faint sigh, and locked.

What would the woman have done if it had been empty? Used an elbow? A nose? Put the files down, sensibly, and used her finger? Amused at the vision she had conjured up, Clemmie felt her nerves begin to recede.

Eleven. The doors opened and a shaft of sunlight pierced the interior darkness. The woman stepped busily out.

A thank you would have been nice, Clemmie thought, before the doors slid shut and she was alone again.

… Sixteen… seventeen… eighteen.

She drew a deep breath. Here it was. Her destiny. Well, her new job, at least.

She stared at the thick glass door that led into the offices of Pruitt and Golding and realised that her heart was pounding in anticipation.

Breathe, she reminded herself.

She breathed.

That's better. First day jitters, that's all.

She never used to be like this – frightened of shadows. Mark had made her this way.

Thinking of Mark filled her with anger and the surge of adrenalin that came with the feeling lent her enough strength to shove at the door, with its opaque decal and smart P&G logo. She would *not* allow her ex to undermine her confidence any longer. It had been a year now, and anyway, no-one here knew anything about it. And this, Clemmie reminded herself sternly, was her dream job at last.

I can do it, she told herself.

She squared her shoulders, ran a ringless hand over her thick dark hair in a vain attempt to tidy it, and forced a smile onto her face as she started towards the receptionist, her heels click-clacking on the dark grey slate floor.

"Hi!"

The youth glanced up. He looked barely seventeen, with his long, carefully unkempt Harry Styles haircut and skin so fresh she wouldn't be surprised if he wasn't even shaving yet. He was neat and slim, and the silky black tee shirt he was wearing was beautifully cut – obviously a designer label.

"You must be Clemmie da Silva. Hi, welcome to Pruitt and Golding."

My goodness, seventeen or not, he was well polished. Either he'd been well trained or he was naturally polite – Clemmie suspected a combination of both. She waved aside the prejudices she'd been ready to cosset and decided that she liked him. A receptionist was the first point of contact for any visitor, so it was important to give the right impression – and the impression she was getting of Pruitt and Golding was of sophistication combined with warmth. A heady combination.

Tick.

"I'm Clemmie, yes." Good, her voice sounded relaxed. She'd been worried about squeaking. All the way here she'd been think about Hope's coaching: breathe, lower your voice an octave, smile when you speak. Her sister was an actress, she knew what she was talking about. "Nice to meet you—" She squinted as unobtrusively as she could at the neat brushed steel and black name badge pinned on his chest. "—Rupert."

The grin seemed genuine. Rupert stood up. Not jeans, she noticed, neatly pressed black trousers and – surprise! – bright scarlet patent leather shoes with pointed toes.

He noticed the direction of her gaze and his smile widened. "I'll show you to Rafa's room. He's expecting you."

She shouldn't be surprised at his choice of work attire. This was a design agency, after all, one of the best in London. Designers like to express their individuality. She loved that Rupert had the confidence – but then again, who didn't, at seventeen?

Clemmie glanced down at her own rather demure navy shift dress and began to worry that she looked middle aged. She certainly didn't look individual enough. She hadn't known what to wear, she'd been in a complete dither until Hope had picked the dress out of her wardrobe with an exasperated, "Oh, for heaven's sake, Clems, play safe on your first day, you can't go wrong with this."

The open plan office they were walking through

had maybe two dozen work stations, mostly sporting large-screen, gleaming Apple Macs. Instantly, her anxieties began to fade. This was safe territory. Clemmie da Silva had been mucking around on Macs since she was ten, she adored the computers with their intuitive software and elegant appearance and there was little she didn't know about them, or the various design programmes she used.

You can do this, she reminded herself, *that's why they've given you the job.*

At the far end of the large office there was a glass-walled meeting room. She could see a dozen people in there, not sitting round the table, but gazing at what appeared to be large pieces of wallpaper stuck on the walls with Blu-tack.

"They're having a brown paper," Rupert said, noticing her curious gaze.

"I'm sorry?"

"We call it a brown paper, but I think they've actually used lining paper this time. Rafa's been having some decorating done at home, he had some spare rolls."

They were nearing the room.

"Don't worry," he added, maybe sensing her anxiety, "it's just a bit of fun. You'll see. But it can be a great creative tool. Rafa's a brilliant facilitator."

Rafael Golding, he meant. The *legendary* Rafael Golding, winner of at least twelve *Design Week* national awards for branding, packaging and graphic design. She was going to meet him at last.

They stood for a moment at the door and listened as a deep, rich voice came from somewhere in the centre of the mêlée.

"Now that you've all had time to take a good look at the ideas, I want you to pick up a sheet of red dots and grade them. You can put three dots on your favourite, two on the second and one for something you think has potential. None on any of the others."

Clemmie could almost feel the excitement as a buzz of conversation began to rise. The voice added warningly, "*Gemma*, I saw that," and the chatter gave way to an eruption of laughter.

And then she saw him.

He was half perched, his back to her, on one corner of the large glass table. His shoulders were wide, his hips slim, his shirt impossibly white, his hair implausibly black. He radiated ease; he was a man undoubtedly in control. He had a pen threaded between his fingers and he was flipping it effortlessly in and out, up and down, round and round as he coolly assessed which images were amassing dots.

Clemmie's heart moved up a beat. Here he was. *The great man.*

It wasn't until he turned that her anticipation turned to disappointment – because he was every romantic novel's heroic stereotype: tall, dark and handsome, with a mane of raven-black hair, dark eyes with impossibly long lashes, and a generous mouth.

No. Surely not. Surely there couldn't be another guy on this planet as good looking as Mark Stanfield – and surely, even if there were, life could not be so cruel as to put him in her path. Because Clemmie da Silva had decided, absolutely and utterly and completely – she had *sworn* in fact – that she could never trust a handsome man again.

"Give me broken noses," she'd said to Hope, "give me crooked teeth and lopsided mouths. Features like that show character. People with odd features have to work hard to make their way in life, they don't go around having everything *fall into their laps* because of the way they look," she'd finished with some bitterness.

"Well, only up to a point," Hope had pointed out in a tone of utter reasonableness. "I mean, even great looking guys can be shy. Or clumsy maybe. Or, like, really rubbish at doing stuff."

"Not in my experience," Clemmie pronounced with a tone of finality. "Trouble is, they can be all those things, but they can still get away with it. And anyway, I wasn't talking about being clumsy or shy. I was talking about being able to attract women like moths to candlelight. And when they've fluttered in, innocently seeking warmth, being utterly unable to resist just reaching out and snatching what's on offer."

Hope's brow had wrinkled as she'd peered at Clemmie shortsightedly. "We all know what you've gone through, Clems. But it still doesn't mean they're all like that."

"Huh," Clemmie had snorted and Hope had shut up. She'd known she couldn't win an argument with Clemmie, not this argument at any rate. After all, she had the facts on her side.

Beside her, she sensed Rupert beginning to move towards the great man. Nothing for it, she'd have to be pleasant. She wanted this job after all; she really, really wanted it.

"Hi!" He'd straightened up and was stepping out from the crowd of busy dot-fixers to greet her. "Great to see you. Clemmie, isn't it?"

She took his hand. "Nice to meet you."

His hand enveloped hers and he didn't let it go. The old trick, she thought with contempt. Make you feel as though you're the only person in the room. Too easy. I won't be falling for that one.

She raised her eyes to his and the floor seemed to tilt suddenly under her feet. The depth of his gaze was bottomless. She was skewered by the intensity of it, pulled into those fathomless eyes until she felt herself falling, helpless. For a few seconds – five, ten, how many? – it were as if the world was whirling around them as they stood motionless in the epicenter of a storm.

Oh no you don't.

She tried to steel herself, just as a cry came across the room, "Rafa! Gemma's cheating again!" and a ripple of laughter hit the glass walls and bounced back into the room so that the sound became amplified.

Clemmie snatched her hand away and switched her gaze to the source of the call.

Rafa said calmly, "They're not always as manic as this. We're up for a truly huge contract and we're all on edge. They're just letting off steam." He turned and called, "All right, troops, stop there. One dot or two isn't going to make a great difference. Let's take a look at what's working for you, shall we?"

Clemmie watched, fascinated despite herself at the apparent eagerness with which they clustered round him and hung onto his words.

Over the next few minutes she observed as Rafa Golding led the team through the rest of the exercise. He was good – there was no doubt about that. He thought clearly, knew where he wanted to go, and knew exactly how to get the designers to follow him there. It was either a natural ability to lead – or it was cynical manipulation of people through the deployment of the gift of natural charm.

Mark had been like that.

June, last year. The day had dawned blue and hot. The perfect day for a wedding. *Her* wedding.

"That's the hairdresser here already," she called up the stairs to Hope, skipping to answer the door, eager to get launched on the timetable of activities they had so meticulously planned.

She'd been up for ages, too excited to sleep. The hairdresser was coming at nine, the manicurist at ten thirty. The flowers would be delivered some time before eleven, and she couldn't wait to see her bouquet, the fabulous gathered bunch of lavender and dark crimson roses she'd chosen. The crimson would exactly match her bridesmaids' dresses. Her sister Hope was to be one of them, of course, and her best friend Evelyn the other.

She'd known Evelyn since college. She was everything Clemmie was not. Where Clemmie was curvy and short, Evelyn was tall and naturally slim. Evelyn could eat anything, and did. Frangipane cakes and chocolate – particularly handmade Belgian chocolates – were her favourites, while Clemmie only had to look at such delights to feel another pound slide onto her hips. Where Clemmie wore her heart on her sleeve, weeping over sad movies and getting emotional about every slight misfortune that beset her friends, Evelyn remained outwardly unmoved. She was kindness itself, of course, but she never cried.

Where *was* Evelyn?

Clemmie opened the door to let the hairdresser in, and glanced at her watch. Her second bridesmaid should have been here by now. She'd wanted her to stay over last night, just to be sure, because you never knew, the roads might be busy, her car might break down, anything could happen, and it was better to be safe than sorry. But Evelyn had said no, that she ought to stay at home with her mother overnight because she'd been poorly and now that she was on her own...

So kind. That was Evelyn all over.

Never mind, she'd be here soon.

"Come in," she said to Angie, the hairdresser. "I've just made coffee. Like a cup? Hope!" she called again, too impatient to get on with the day to wait for an answer. "Mum! We have lift off!"

Her hair was never easy to manage. It was thick and naturally curly. But they'd had a dry run and Angie knew exactly what she had to do. Hope envied Clemmie's hair, but her own was much easier to manage, and all her mother needed was a wash and blow dry, with a little extra spray so that it wouldn't be too squashed by her hat.

Caught up in it all, she forgot about Evelyn until she emerged from the drier, a little red in the face and desperate to get on with the next item on her list. The flowers arrived and were perfect. The lavender was the deepest of purpley blue, the roses

– *thank goodness* – were the exact colour of the bridesmaids' dresses – she'd worried they might be too pale.

Bridesmaids! Evelyn!

She grabbed her phone and texted rapidly: *"Where are U?"*

There was no answer.

"Ready for your nails?" The manicurist had arrived and was waiting, her polishes and files spread out in front of her in a neat array.

"In a minute."

Clemmie texted again. *"Hairdresser about to GO! R u OK? Has something happened?"*

Then she was stuck, with her hands outstretched, as the shellac was applied, but she watched her phone, worry starting to turn to panic as it remained silent.

"Calm down, Clems," Hope said. "If the worst comes to the worst, you still have me. You're not going to be bridesmaidless."

"Oh, Hope," Clemmie wailed as tears threatened, "I know I do, and don't think I don't appreciate it, but I really, really want Evelyn to be here too."

At half past twelve, she allowed herself to be coaxed into her dress – the gorgeous, ivory silk creation she'd picked out with Evelyn on a trip to London. She cried "Ouch!" out of habit as Hope pulled in the laces at the back of the bodice to nip in her waist, but actually, she barely felt their effect.

"You've lost a load of weight, Clems," Hope commented, standing back to admire her sister. "That diet's been terrific."

Clemmie glanced in the mirror. She looked almost waif-like, thanks to the flattering lines of the dress and her recent efforts.

"Lovely," she said abstractedly, looking across at the clock. "But where the hell is Evelyn?"

As if to answer her question, the doorbell trilled, its ring harsh.

"That'll be her. Thank goodness! I hope she's at least washed her hair because Angie's gone already. We'll just have to do the best we can."

"I'll go," Hope said, moving towards the door.

But Clemmie was off already, excitement and relief making her skip down the stairs in eager anticipation.

She wrenched the door open. "Hi, Evelyn. What happened— Oh!"

Clemmie gasped in astonishment. Evelyn was standing on the doorstep looking grey and nervous, and behind her stood... Mark.

"You can't see me like this," Clemmie gasped. "Go away! It's bad luck to see the bride on the morning of the wedding. Shoo!"

She reached out for Evelyn's hand to haul her inside, but Evelyn jerked it away.

"No, Clems, sorry. We need to talk to you."

"Talk to me? What about? Has something happened? It's not your mother, is it? Oh, Evelyn—" Clemmie could feel tears rising to her eyes. If Evelyn's mother was worse... been rushed to hospital... died... today of all days...

"It's not Mum." Evelyn was mumbling, her head was down, she wasn't even looking at Clemmie.

Mark spoke. "Clemmie, we do need to come in. Sorry."

Clemmie looked at him then. There was something in his voice that didn't sound right. He didn't sound like the loving, easy-going man she'd known for years, he sounded tense and agitated. Cold fear began to creep into her bones. Something clearly *had* happened. Something dreadful.

She opened the door silently and allowed them to step inside.

"Rafa's wonderful, isn't he?"

It was her second week at Pruitt and Golding, and already Clemmie had made friends. Making this comment was Eleanor, the designer she shared a workstation with. Eleanor was a skinny scrap of a girl. She favoured black, wore huge quantities of kohl and dark shadow, and sprayed a lock of her dark hair a different colour every day. Today it was a green that was almost fluorescent. She was a brilliant designer, and clients loved her bubbly personality. Clemmie had already learned lots from her.

"Wonderful?" she queried.

Clemmie found Rafael Golding unsettling. She'd barely spoken to him since that first encounter, but every time he walked across the room to talk to someone, she felt compelled to compare him with Mark. After all, they shared that easy acceptance of the good looks that made them naturally attractive. They were both charming and they both played down their charm. Mark had always been the centre of admiring groups of women at parties, heads turned when he walked down the street – and she'd always been so proud to be with him, ecstatic that she'd been the one he'd chosen.

Idiot.

Eleanor said, "You know, everyone adores him but he's so kind. He takes time to mentor and encourage people, even though he's under such pressure himself."

Easy to do.

Easy to make people trust you.

"And even though he's so busy, he always makes time to spend with his girl."

Clemmie spied Rafa making his way across the office to them now, even as Eleanor's words sank in.

His girl.

Boy, why was she so disappointed? Hadn't she been absolutely determined not to let good looks attract her ever again? But on the half dozen or so occasions she had encountered Rafa Golding over the last few days, she'd found herself unaccountably shaken by the feelings he aroused in her.

Idiot, she mocked herself again, this time for a very different reason. Or was it the same reason?

She had trusted Mark absolutely. After all, they'd been together since sixth year – almost twelve years. She knew him inside out, or thought she did. She knew that he adored steak pie and hated olives, that he'd never been drunk since the final year dance when he'd made a complete idiot of himself in a club and vowed never to repeat the experience. She knew that he left his socks on the floor and spatters of toothpaste all over the bathroom mirror, and that he had a birthmark on the inside of his right thigh just where—

Stop!

Whatever.

She knew him well enough, she'd thought, to

entrust her happiness to him. Until the day of their wedding. Until the day that he'd arrived on her doorstep with Evelyn Barker, her *best friend* and told her that he couldn't marry her, that Evelyn was moving in with him – moving in to the house *she* had so lovingly decorated and furnished – that he was sorry he hadn't had the courage to tell her sooner.

"*Sorry!*" she exclaimed, her voice replete with indignant fury.

"What are you sorry for?" said an amused voice.

Clemmie looked up. Rafa was standing right in front of her, smiling the impossibly bright smile that transformed his classically symmetrical features from the brooding expression she'd sometimes observed into something almost warm.

"Oh!" She jumped up, almost knocking over her coffee mug and perilously close to sending coffee flying over the designs she'd just done for the pitch she was working on.

"Steady," Rafa said, laying a hand on her arm. "I didn't mean to alarm you."

Clemmie looked round, but Eleanor had wandered away to talk to someone across the room, leaving her alone with Rafa Golding.

"Sorry," Clemmie said again, not knowing what else to say. This was silly. "Do you want something?" she demanded. Then, realising this might sound rude, rephrased the question. "I mean, is there something I can do for you?"

It seemed to Clemmie that his grin was too smooth, too practised. "Actually, I was wondering whether you might like to come out for a drink after work? We could talk about your first couple of weeks. I'd like to know how you feel you're settling in."

"Ah... Oh..." Clemmie stuttered, surprised, before anger got the better of her. He was asking her out for a drink when his girl would be waiting at home? Probably with a lovely supper on the table, wine chilling in the fridge, maybe candles waiting to be lit? How could he? Typical, she thought, her anger turning to fury. Handsome men? Pah!

"No," she said. "Sorry. I'm not free."

"Oh." He looked surprised. There – that had jolted him. He probably wasn't used to women turning down his offers. From what she'd seen at the office, there was barely a woman in the place who wouldn't leap at the chance of a date, not unattached ones, at any rate.

"Another time then," he said smoothly, before lifting up one of her designs and assessing it as though nothing had happened.

That couldn't have been disappointment she'd glimpsed in those inky black eyes, could it?

Nonsense. He'd just been taken aback, that's all.

Well, that would teach him. Not every woman under the sun fell for his undoubted charms – the sensible ones certainly didn't.

Hope's reaction to the story, when she recounted it later that evening, was a surprise.

"Why don't you give him a chance?" she asked, one eyebrow raised interrogatively.

"A *chance*? Hope!"

"Just because he's a handsome guy like Mark doesn't mean—"

"But I told you, he has a girl at home. There's only one kind of guy who'd ask someone out in those circumstances and it's not the sort I want to be with. Not ever again."

"It was just a drink," Hope said reasonably.

"You think? You should have seen the way he looked at me."

Hope swished tea around in her mug. She was "resting" at the moment, looking for another role. She hated it when she was out of work, but Clemmie secretly loved having her sister around. After the year she'd had, it was fantastic to have someone at hand she could really rely on. Hope said, thoughtfully, "Don't rush to judgement, Clems. Give the guy a chance."

Clemmie said nothing. She couldn't believe that Hope was taking Rafa's side – and she hadn't even met him.

"We won!"

"Isn't it brilliant?"

"Hope they'll let me stay on now." This from a young work experience graduate who was hoping for a permanent post.

"Clemmie, they used your designs, didn't they? Clever you! Rafa'll be all over you."

All over you. No doubt. That would be Rafael Golding's style, she imagined. But it wouldn't work with her.

At the end of the day, someone appeared with champagne and they all celebrated. It was her first taste of success, and Clemmie found herself toasted again and again.

"Brilliant!"

"I loved your designs, Clemmie."

"Well done!"

She perched on the corner of a desk and held court, savouring the sweet flavour of professional triumph. She didn't notice she'd been boxed into a corner by the crowd, so when Rafa slid between two print buyers in the throes of an animated discussion and tipped some bubbly into her glass there were no avenues open for escape.

"How does it feel," he asked, his gaze searing into her like a branding iron, "to be a key cog in the wheel of our success?"

Don't. Clemmie was in danger of losing control of her feelings and began to panic.

Don't look at me like that. It isn't fair.

"I'm very happy," she replied truthfully, her heart fluttering.

"Happy enough," he lowered his voice so that she could only just hear him above the hubbub, "to have dinner with me?"

She summoned all her strength. "You're very kind," she replied, politely formal, "but I fear you may have the wrong idea about me."

His eyes flickered and she saw him stiffen.

"Okay. I can take a hint," he said, his lips twisting into a wry smile. "I won't ask again, Clementine." He began to turn away.

"My name isn't Clementine," she said, out of force of habit, because all her life, everyone had jumped to the wrong conclusion.

But he just shrugged and pushed his way back through the throng. In an instant, he had gone.

Over the next few months, Clemmie's impression of Rafa Golding was continually reinforced. He was excellent at his job – brilliant, in fact. He had natural appeal. He was great with the clients, supportive of the staff. Everyone adored him. The women, in particular, flocked around him.

Could no-one see him for what he really was? Had no-one else experienced the duplicity she'd glimpsed?

Clemmie kept her head down and got on with her work – Pruitt and Golding really was everything she had hoped for in an employer and then some. Harvey Pruitt, a pleasant-looking man in his mid-fifties, greying but well turned out, provided the perfect counterweight to Rafa Golding's flamboyant charm. Her colleagues were, by and large, pleasant, the work was constantly stimulating and challenging, and she'd made a number of quite good friends already.

Eleanor said one morning, "Are you coming to the abseil tomorrow?"

"Abseil?" Clemmie said absently, refreshing her screen. "What abseil?"

"Surely you've heard about it? Rafa's abseiling off the building in aid of Movember. Everyone's turning out. You'll chip in, won't you?"

"What's Movember?" Clemmie swivelled round in her chair and looked at Eleanor, now all attention.

"The charity for men's health," Eleanor said. "Of course, Rafa's a terrific supporter of it."

"Of course?"

Eleanor swept back her hair – the coloured strand was tangerine today. "Since his father died of prostate cancer."

"Oh! That's terrible."

"Well, coming right after his wife's death it hit him really hard."

Clemmie's heart kick started from seventy beats a minute to something over a hundred and sixty. "His wife died?" she stuttered. "When was that?"

Eleanor shrugged. "Two years ago? It's been really hard for him."

Two years only? And already he had another girl? Grief hadn't lasted long; he'd gone out and found someone else with indecent haste.

"So are you coming?" Eleanor was saying. "His little girl will be there."

Clemmie stared at her. "His what?"

"His little girl. Lily. I told you he spends as much time as he can with her. Rafa's mum's going to bring her along. At least she's old enough now to appreciate what he's doing."

"L-Lily."

Had she been unbelievably stupid? She remembered Hope's words: "Don't rush to judgement."

"Yup. Pretty name, huh? She must be… what – eight by now?"

"Lily's his daughter?"

Eleanor was looking at her oddly. "Sure."

"And 'his girl'? His only girl?"

"What's got into you, Clemmie? Rafa's only had time for Lily since his wife died. He could have any girl in this office…" – she swept an expressive arm from side to side, encompassing the entire room – "…but he's never been out with anyone, not that we know of, since she passed away. And then with his dad dying too… Well, he dedicated all his spare time to fundraising and child rearing. And running the business, of course." She sighed. "He must be such a lovely dad."

Clemmie's heart was skipping and jumping. What a fool she'd been! What an utter idiot.

"Tomorrow?" she said.

"Midday. Twenty-four floors and he's sliding down from the top." Eleanor shook her head admiringly. "Mad. But an absolute angel, don't you think?"

It was a typical November day: clear and bright, but frosty. Clemmie was wearing her bright-red winter coat and a stripey wool scarf. She couldn't bear to stand with the others – she knew she'd be too emotional and she didn't want them to read the wrong things into that. It was just… well, just that she was beginning to admire Rafael Golding. That was all. So she stood at the side of the plaza, close to the fountain, all alone.

She looked up. And up. And up. Right at the very top of the gleaming glass building, she could just see two figures – Rafa presumably, and the abseiling expert, clipping him in.

He was going to do it! He was going to slide all the way down that glass cliff. For charity. Even if it was her mother dying, or her sister Hope, there was no way she could bring herself to do it. No way.

She shivered. It wasn't just the cold; it was fear – for Rafa's safety.

Beside her, the crowd was swelling. At the front,

she saw a small figure holding the hand of an elderly lady with a shock of pure white hair. Rafa's mother and his daughter presumably.

How could she have misjudged him so badly? She'd got everything wrong.

She spied a figure clambering over the edge of the building. How terrified was he, at this moment? Clemmie felt sick.

And then he was hurtling through the air, leaping and bouncing against the building, jumping, releasing, bouncing again.

A huge cheer went up. He was on the ground at last.

Clemmie stood stock still, a lone figure, set apart from the crowd. He wouldn't see her. Why would he, when he'd only have eyes for his daughter? She'd blown it, thrown away a chance for happiness because of her own stubbornness.

She watched as Rafa was unhooked from his ropes. He started walking across the plaza, towards his family.

And then a miracle happened.

He changed direction.

He started walking towards her!

She stood, trembling – It's just the cold, she told herself – and waiting.

"Hello, not Clementine," he said quietly when he was near enough. His eyes were fizzing with excitement, he was still high on adrenaline. Gone was the charm she had believed was artificial – this was real!

"That was well done," she said, her eyes bright with unshed tears. "You're very brave."

"I enjoyed it." He nodded and started to turn.

Don't go!

"My name is Clemency," she blurted out, before she could think about what she was saying.

He turned back. "Clemency?"

"I hate it. I've always hated it." She pursed her lips together for a moment, then said, "It means mercy, or forgiveness. But I'm the one who should be asking for clemency. I've misjudged you."

He nodded, expressionless.

Clemmie felt her face burning, despite the cold. *Damn, damn, damn!* She'd made such a fool of herself.

Rafa held out his hand. "You're forgiven, Clemency. Come on. There's someone I'd like you to meet."

Her heart skipped at his touch. Hope had been right – she should not have condemned Raphael just because of Mark.

Learning how to trust again might not be an easy journey to make, but it looked as though she might have her very own archangel to guide her along the way.

The End

Jenny   Harper lives in Edinburgh. She is the author of four books about Scotland and Scottish culture, a history of childbirth, and *The Sleeping Train* for young readers. When she isn't writing, she enjoys walking in the Scottish countryside or anywhere warm, and travel to Europe, America and India.

"Nothing in life is simple, and my books tackle the many and often complex issues that affect the modern woman. Themes such as challenging careers, friendship, trust and betrayal, ambition and grief lie at the heart of my novels. My heroines have to work out what's really important and make difficult choices. There's love too, of course, and heroes who have pasts of their own...

I write about strong women under pressure and I'm fascinated by predicaments, lies, secrets and language."

Website: jennyharperauthor.co.uk
FB: www.facebook.com/authorjennyharper
Twitter: twitter.com/harper_jenny

THE LETTER
by Nikki Mason

He stared at the words in his hands. The letters swirled and swooped more elegantly than he remembered. Hard to make out if he didn't know their meaning by heart. Hours he'd spent tracing the lines with his fingers, gorging them with his eyes, these words that were once hers but were now his. In his mind. In his soul. They spoke of a lost time. Before his skin was papery and dour. Before his mind began to grow feeble. Before he'd even married.

Now the words began to blur, the familiar writing becoming unfocused as tears threatened to spill over his drooping eyelids. This was the last time he'd know her. They were moving him out, away from his home and all the possessions that made up him and his life. That made up who he was. He was once the receiver of this letter – adored, wanted and vital. He once ran with vigour, lusted to touch this woman's skin which was covered in freckles brought out by the sun.

He had laid her down in a field of wildflowers, away from the watchful grey eyes of her ever-frowning mother. He had kissed her petulant mouth, plump and full and cherry red. She'd stop sulking and giggled at the way his moustache tickled her face, before dissolving, her warm, supple body becoming pliant in his hands.

"I'm yours, Tom," she'd whispered that last time, her heart locking with his. "Mother and father

142

will just have to live with it."

She had been so sure that he, a mere farmhand turned Private, heading off to war, was the right man for her. A beauty, an heiress, an innocent. He had held her tighter, kissing her again, making her feel loved, but he'd never fully be able to express the way his soul ached for hers, his firm, youthful body made frail and unsure when he caught a glimpse of her.

He saw the way the staff at her grand house sneered at him as he waited outside. And once he'd caught a glimpse of a handsome gent entering the house, clutching twelve clichéd red roses. He'd straightened his spine but refused to move from his post – she was expecting him. He'd only been able to give her buttercups, rich in name but common weeds. He saw the motorcars, the trays laden with rich fruit cake, with china, with... goodness only knew.

"Hang it," he'd said, releasing her waist.

"Tom?"

How could he degrade her to bread and dripping, off cuts, handouts, a hard working life? And who knew, maybe he wouldn't come back from France and she'd be left with a pittance and shame. She'd be ashamed to have his name.

With tears rising in his eyes, he traced her wonderfully soft lips with his finger, stood and saluted, and turned away.

"Tom!"

He turned back and looked at her still lying there, so beautiful.

"I love you," he choked, before striding away up the hill, away from love, away from safety, towards his destiny. She hadn't understood.

A week later on the train down to Bristol, he still felt the firmness of his lips pressing hers.

Now his lips were puckered and thin, their redness faded to an unsightly mauve, but always hers would be youthful and smiling. Just as her letter would always be new, full of questions, longing and hope.

But the questions he had left unanswered, and he had left her hope to diminish. He'd had to stay strong… though he felt anything but now. What was strength? Was walking away strength? Was choosing to spear men with bayonets over love the decision of a hero?

He sat down heavily at his cheap pine table and took up his pen. With hands that shook, he finally responded. His heart full and sure, despite a lifetime of uncertainty. Now he knew what he had to do, now before they took him away. He smiled as he wrote. His letters crooked and scratchy. Their meaning known by heart.

The End

Nikki Mason is a journalist, actress and fiction editor at CandleLit Author Services. She frequently writes fiction herself and enjoys playing with flash fiction and the challenge of cramming as much emotion as possible into the smaller form. Nikki currently lives, writes and bakes in West Yorkshire with her man and her kitten.

Twitter: twitter.com/nikcasartelli
Website: candlelitauthorservices.com
Blog: nikkicasartelli.wordpress.com

A BIT LIKE BRIDGET JONES
by Zara Stoneley

Friday 24th October
Sophie
9 a.m.

OMG, the sex god spoke to me! I am in love. Well, lust. Well, whatever. He just has to be the most gorgeous man ever, well, in real life. I have always fancied Henry Cavill, and that guy who was Aragorn in *Lord of the Rings*, and then there is Richard Armitage when he looks all stern and unforgiving. But I do realise that they could be a complete let down in real life, although if any of them would actually like to call me, I'd be prepared to take the risk and find out.

I've been eyeing him up (sex god, not Henry Cavill) over the top of my e-reader for several months, but he's never actually acknowledged me before. Never actually caught me doing it (or if he had he was too polite to make it obvious). Commuter relationships are a bit like speed dating, without the drinks, or the chat. You sit down, try not to stare too obviously, and then rush off when the train pulls into your stop. I see more of sex god than I see my mother, so I do feel we almost have a relationship. And as I do not want a proper relationship yet, sex god has been my ideal date.

He has no wedding ring (good), a dimple (excellent, lots of sex gods have dimples), dark curly hair that always looks slightly ruffled (good, definitely not too much man grooming going on), open-necked shirt and nice suit (cheap suits are tacky but this one suggests he is a man of adequate means, and the open-neck means he's not stuffy; stuffy suits and I aren't compatible).

I thought Sam was gorgeous (before he dumped me and went off with the laughing hyena), but I've realised he wasn't. I obviously didn't have very high standards when I met him; something my mother tells me off for. Well, she was right. And I have upped my standards since starting train speed dating. I have met a sex god.

I was just having a sneak peek as I went on to a new page and he winked. Well, I hope it was a wink. Oh hell, what if it was a nervous twitch? No, he didn't look the type to be nervous about anything. Sam was nervous about all kinds of things. Like my driving. I mean, what is it about men that means they can drive at well over the speed limit, and simultaneously make rude gestures at people, whereas if I as much as lean out to look at a cat stuck up a tree they're reaching over to grab the steering wheel? I am perfectly capable of driving. Quite well, in fact. And statistically women are much safer drivers than men are.

I ignored him, read the page quickly, and when I started the next one he was still looking my way.

"*Fifty Shades?*" He had that slightly upper class edge to his voice that made me think about afternoon tea and champagne. Oh God, that's it! I've met my Mr Darcy, now all I need is that lake… "Or are you into more serious stuff?" He nodded pointedly in the direction of my Kindle, which was now plastered to my nose.

"Sorry, yes, I mean no. I mean not *Fifty Shades*. Oh no, no, that's so passé now." I don't want him to think I'm a sex maniac, do I? "We aren't all into whips and er, stuff."

"Really?"

Did I detect a note of disappointment? Or does he now think I am a sex maniac and trying to hide the fact? I decided to take the high ground so I don't appear sluttish. "That isn't a very original chat-up line, you know."

"Chat-up line?"

"Oh." He wasn't chatting me up. Oh hell, what do I say now? And it is actually *Fifty Shades*, and I must be the very last person on earth to read it. My mother made me, she said it might help. Haven't got a clue what she means. But that is the trouble with books like this: one minute you're a sane, newly (and happily) single girl and the next you're thinking about whips and bondage. And all men who see you reading a book assume you are too. As if we have nothing better to think about.

"My stop." And then he winked. Again. At me. And grinned. "Enjoy the rest of your book."

"Thank you. It's a serious book. A... murder mystery type of thing." Murder? Mystery? Where did that come from? Now he'll think I'm into axe wielding lunatics, or I am one.

"And you're absolutely not into whips?"

I shook my head.

"Shame."

So what exactly did he mean by that? Maybe I've missed my big chance and I should have run after him, and jumped off the train yelling: "Whip me, whip me. I'll try anything once."

I was seriously tempted for a second, but the conductor had blown his whistle and I'd probably end up with one foot on the train and one off, desperately running along trying not to die.

It put me off *Fifty Shades* a bit, so I turned my e-reader off, but held it up so that other people would still think I was engrossed.

I tried to take my mind off the fact that I'd missed my ONE BIG CHANCE by reading over the shoulder of the man next to me. But he kept harrumphing and shaking the magazine as though he knew. And it looked boring anyway. Some FTSE nonsense, which I used to think was footsie, when I was young. I made the mistake of mentioning it at the dinner table and it got added to my father's repertoire of funny stories to recount in public, only to be forgotten after I'd confused Cardiff and Carlisle and headed up the M6 the wrong way when I was going to Alice's wedding. I got there just after the speeches, which I actually see as a bonus.

It was easier when I used to travel on the Tube. Nobody looks at you properly there. I once read a whole article about moon phases over this girl's shoulder without her knowing. And I could tell that the full moon thing bothered her. She kept flicking back and reading it again.

And another time I read several pages of this really sad love story, and we'd just got to the bit where she told him she had this incurable disease and it would make her old and ugly, and she wanted him to remember her as perfect and... the silly woman switched to some story about a man and a dog, or a man in a boat. Actually, I think it was about a man and a dog in a boat.

Mr Darcy did wink at me though (henceforth he shall be known as Mr Darcy; much more becoming than sex god). Maybe this is how it's all going to start. Me, Miss Left-on-the-Shelf, is going to find true love on the daily commute into Manchester. And everybody will be so jealous.

Note to self: skip through book and find the filthy bits in case he is here again and wants to discuss them.

I nearly forgot to get off the train at my stop and had to make a mad dash for the door. Visions of doing the running thing and dying an unromantic death with no Mr Darcy to save me. Recovering with coffee and half a bar of chocolate that I found hidden in the zipped-up pocket of my bag. (Why do they have those compartments? All you do is forget what you've put in there.)

Hannah is doing that looking-over-her-glasses thing, which means she's realised that I've not been doing the work she asked for. I think she's got some kind of telepathic thing going on. I did try concentrating on her hard and blocking her out, but she asked if I'd got a squint.

9:30 a.m.
Trying to remember just what Mr Darcy had said to me and work out what I should say to him next time I see him. Is it forward to start a conversation?

"Nearly finished, Sophie? Or are we day dreaming about George Clooney again?" Oops, Hannah had snuck up and was glaring over her glasses at me. I hate that sarcastic, superior tone.

"I was trying to think of the best phrasing, and…" – I paused for effect – "…George Clooney is too old for me." At least my hands are over the keyboard.

"You're writing an advert for a second-hand car sales business. And..." – she paused to annoy me – "...George Clooney is not too old for anybody."

"Pre-loved." I like the word pre-loved. Second-hand sounds like nobody wants it. "The cars are pre-loved." And George Clooney *is* too old for me, even my mother fancies him. I would have said it out aloud, but she was giving me "the look".

Friday 24th October
Dave
8:45 a.m.
Text to Gary Hopper: *"No."*

Text from Gary Hopper: *"Most blokes would jump at the chance."*

Text to Gary Hopper: *"Get one of them to do it then."*

Text from GazBag: *"They don't get paid to. You do."*

I'd got bored and changed his name in my contacts list. There are worse things I could have called him. Lots worse.

8:46 a.m.
Gary, otherwise known as GazBag, was standing in front of my desk, a cup of coffee in each hand. He plonked one down, obviously a peace offering.

"It's only a month out of your life."

Not a peace offering. A bribe.

"I'll sleep on it."

"You could be sleeping on something, or somebody, else by the end of next month if you get it

151

right." He smirked.

8:51 a.m.
What Do Women Want?
How Hirsute Do You Want Your Hero?
Is Hairy Hot?
Cack. I deleted all three headings (which looked worse on the screen than they had in my head) and sat back, nursing the plastic cup of lukewarm dishwater – sorry, coffee – and drummed my fingers on the keyboard until Josie sent a polite cough in my direction. It always started polite, then led to something bordering on GBH if you annoyed her too much. I reckon it was only the fact that Gary harboured a secret desire to be dominated that stopped him accusing her of sexual harassment. He lived in hope, as we all do.

"Am I growing on you?"

"Sorry?" My laptop screen was splattered with a generous coating of second-hand coffee as the dominatrix spoke scary words. Shit, no way was I going there. Ever.

"I said, am I growing on you? For your title, you stupid twat. Christ!" She rolled her eyes, which was some feat given the good layer of black around her eyes and the spikes on her eyelids. They always reminded me of those furry caterpillars and I had a horrible fascination with them. One day they'd break loose and start to walk across her face. "Where does he get them from?"

I took that as the derogatory comment it was meant to be. And was wise enough not to comment.

She fixed me with a glare that would have done a

weasel proud. "You didn't honestly think I was coming on to you?"

I shrugged. "Well, I have been told I'm irresistible."

"By your mother, or in your dreams?"

My day would come.

Am I Growing On You Yet?

Yeah, it looked good. "You're a genius." I'd long since decided that the approach of the other guys to wind her up by using endearments was a no-hoper. She looked smug, and left me alone. Result.

10:30 a.m.

There are days when you just need the weekend to come along and save you. Not even lunch time. So near and yet so far.

I wasn't sure I was the right guy to try and figure out what went on in a girl's head. My only hope was the girl on the train. The 7:36 which had more stops than any train had the right to between home and work. Although why the hell I'd mentioned *Fifty Shades* this morning I do not know. Has my ability to talk to a woman been reduced to innuendoes? I had quite a nifty turn of chat-up lines at one time, or maybe I just imagined it. Maybe in the cruel light of day, without the aid of a packed bar and a pint or two, I am crap at talking to the opposite sex.

At least she'd have plenty of opportunity to call me a weirdo and bolt for the exit (if she can get past my suggestion that her reading matter is mass-market, sexually orientated women's stuff). And the whole project had been my idea in the first place, just not this particular aspect. Whichever way I looked at it, GazBag knew he had me by the short and curlies.

Let the train take the strain.

7 p.m.
"So?" I took a long, hard slug of the pint of bitter, and gave him my best stare. He was unimpressed. Women are much better at scary looks than men.

"I need to know, if *you* don't do it then somebody else gets your column for the month."

I knew he didn't mean it. He'd said it before.

"It's deceitful."

"Bollocks."

"I could get a slap in the face."

"Or a kick in the nuts; just the type of copy we need. I can see the strapline now: *Lose Your Manhood for Movember*." He looked pleased with himself.

"Thanks. Your headlines are crap. And what if I get arrested?"

For an intelligent man, Gary came up with some stupid ideas, and this had to be is best yet. My daily column was to be taken over for the month of November in aid of Movember. Great idea so far (mine), awareness, social conscience and all that jazz. In fact, although I can be flippant it actually was worthwhile.

But Gary had to add his own spin on everything, good or bad. His contribution had been to suggest (interpret suggest as diktat) that I find out if a random stranger (preferably female) would find me more or less attractive as each day passed, as my moustache took over my face and made me resemble a hobbit's foot. At what point would she be repelled? And what would she do? Or would she be able to see past the furry slug? Is Movember a guy's thing (well, obviously as far as the facial hair growth it is), or do women actually like it?

I think he was losing the point a bit, as well as the plot.

Problem one: finding a woman who found me attractive. Problem two: finding a woman who found me attractive and I saw each day. Problem three: finding a woman who found me attractive, I saw each day and who wouldn't put me in hospital when she realised she was newspaper fodder.

"It's for a good cause."

I studied the froth moustache that Gary was now supporting. Unattractive. "It could take me all month to find someone who will let me kiss her." Two months once the growth gets underway.

"Good man, I knew you'd do it. Another pint?"

Monday 27th October
Sophie
9 a.m.

Our speed dating has moved up to a new level. I really think this could be the way forward for everybody, meeting in bars or online is so out-dated.

Mr Darcy spoke as soon as he sat down, which means I have not missed my big chance. Playing hard to get is obviously the way to go.

"Hey!"

I'd been dreaming about that voice. It fits the rest of him, so rugged, so masculine. I can remember being totally shocked the first time I heard David Beckham speak (although I did get over it and forgive him as the rest is perfect). But Mr Darcy's voice is just what you would expect from him. I read once that the type of man you fancy varies with your hormones; well, mine are obviously on the not perfectly groomed setting today, along with slightly cultured but deep voice.

I am so glad I did the pink nail varnish, which looks very upmarket when I wrap my hands round my e-reader and tap (in case he hasn't noticed). It made it so bloody hard to press the button for the next page though, I sometimes wish I had double jointed thumbs. By the time I stopped thinking about my newly manicured nails he was staring at his mobile phone and shaking his head.

I've blown it. He's never going to speak to me again. I will have to live with "hey". In fact, he's frowning. He thinks I'm totally deranged.

"*War and Peace*?" Maybe not. The phone has gone back in his pocket and his attention seems to be back on me.

He has got the most gorgeous eyes, and these cute dimples like Colin Firth has. He really is my Mr Darcy. It's a sign.

"Er, no. *Fifty Shades*. I thought I'd do some research on whips, seeing as you were disappointed the other day." God, did I really say that? What's he going to do now? Have I blown my second chance? I'd cross my fingers, but I think my nail varnish has stuck to my e-reader (on the fingers that weren't tapping, obviously). I knew I shouldn't have tried to put it on thirty seconds before I left for work. Normal nail varnish is fine, but ultra-glossy-gel-ly stuff could be a mistake.

"And?"

"I've… er, not reached that bit yet. There's quite a bit of talking and… er, stuff to wade through first."

"You'll have to let me know when you do."

"Sure." I am so pathetic, why can't I say something clever, or mildly amusing?

"I'm Dave, by the way." He held a hand out tentatively as though he wasn't sure if we should shake on that nugget of information. I just smiled, because it was my shaking hand that was stuck, then decided it was better to look silly than rude and stuck out my left one instead.

"I'm stuck." An explanation seemed in order.

"Oh, that's not an English name, is it German?"

"No, I mean I am actually stuck. To this."

He grinned.

"Maybe you shouldn't shake my hand in case you get stuck on me too."

"Would that be a bad thing? Me getting stuck on you? You might get to like it."

I must have looked puzzled, because he shook his head. "Sorry, stupid thing to say."

"No, no, it's not stupid." Quite a nice thing to say, but a bit strange. On the train. In the morning. (I've never really got the sexy in the morning thing, and definitely not on a train. I mean, there's stubble, and bed head, and sweaty bits. Sticky bits actually, now I come to think of it, which I shouldn't be doing.) "Not that you're asking for sex."

"Er, no, I'm not."

"Oh God, did I say that out loud?"

"You did." He looked serious. No wonder, when

a stranger has just practically accused him of demanding sex in the rush hour. I'd never realised that nail varnish could be such a dangerous thing.

"Well, it might not be that bad a thing, apart from, of course, the logistics, you know, of work and everything. If we were stuck together, that is." Somebody shoot me please.

"Can I ask your opinion on something, as a woman?"

This is good; nobody ever asks my opinion on anything... well, men don't. I mean, my best mate does ask if her hair is too red, or her top too low cut, or things like that. But not for a proper opinion. "I'm not very keen on politics."

He laughed. "Thank God for that."

"Or football."

"This isn't deep and meaningful."

"Oh." I felt mildly deflated, even though I hadn't heard the question yet.

"How do you feel about facial hair?" I must have looked alarmed. "Beards, moustaches? Would you prefer kissing somebody with or without?"

"Kissing?"

"Or anything." He grinned. A dirty grin with a raised eyebrow.

"Ah, I'm not sure about the anything." I said, thinking about nasty rashes. "And to be honest," and I did always try to be open and honest, "I've never done it."

"It?" He raised one eyebrow and looked incredibly suggestive, or that could be my dirty mind.

"Kissed someone with a beard, or moustache."

"Oh."

"Although I have done stubble." I wouldn't like

158

him to think me a complete novice, or a virgin.

"But you'd be game to try?"

That sounded rude, and a bit of a come on.

"Oh shoot, my stop." He made a grab for his briefcase, then hesitated, waiting for an answer.

"Maybe."

"Oh, to hell with it!" Then he made a grab for my hand (the one that wasn't stuck) and there was a brief tug-of-war (I'm not used to strange, or even very attractive, men grabbing my hands but he was unexpectedly firm) before his very manly and slightly rough chin brushed over my knuckles as he looked me straight in the eye, and then he dipped his head so that I got this brief whiff of a kind of woody, earthy smell of clean hair before soft dry lips touched my fingers so lightly I could have imagined it.

And he was gone. Before I'd even got chance to say a word. Or ask what the hell he was talking about. I stared down at my reclaimed hand, then out of the window.

And I'm pretty sure that what he mouthed through it was: "Catch you tomorrow", but that could have been wishful thinking. And what did he mean by "game to try"? With him?

Monday 27th October
Dave
8:55 a.m.
Result! She said yes. I think.

I spent most of the journey trying to weigh her up and decide whether she was actually flirting, was just one of those people who stared when they were thinking about their book and I just happened to be in her line of sight, or was nervous. Or desperate to visit the ladies. My musing is interrupted.

Text from Gary: *"Well?"*

Text to Gary Gopher (okay, I'm immature and changed my contact list again, I don't care): *"I haven't a clue what goes through a woman's mind and how I'm going to get through a whole sodding month. What do you think about United's chances of getting a win tomorrow?"*

Text from Gary: *"Knew you'd do it, you dirty dog. Make today's copy funny, get them gagging for it. I'm betting on a draw mate, defence looks crap."*

God knows how that man got to be an editor. Gagging for it?

She was peering over her e-reader at me the second I sat down. Very, very green-brown eyes. In fact, quite like a cat, although she seemed to be turning a shade of pink. It might be my caveman mentality (I do believe that every man has it buried somewhere deep, or not so deep, inside), but it was like a green light. I could do it.

"Would you mind if I—"

Her eyebrows jumped, then she actually lowered the book so that I could see the rest of her face. Very nice lips. First time I'd seen them properly, although had I actually been looking? It was only now that she was possibly a target for snogging that it dawned on me that I really wanted to do it. Snog her.

I'd wanted to for a while, and the more I thought about it, the more I wanted it. But the whole starting up a convo on the train thing wasn't my style. Needs must. Or deadlines must.

Kiss you – it had been on the tip of my tongue. I mean, this exercise required a certain amount of bodily contact, to see if the whole hairy, bristly stage could be overcome. And if I didn't get in quick then we'd be skipping the smooth stage.

She gave me a startled look even though I hadn't actually said it. And I'd been planning just a peck, not a full on snog.

Maybe a handshake was a better idea. I held out a hand and she looked at me like I was a Martian. So much for my assessment of the situation that she was actually interested.

"Sorry, I'm a bit, well, stuck to my—"

What kind of girl gets glued to her belongings? But she was grinning and looking flustered, which was kind of cute. Totally unlike my ex-girlfriend who would have demanded I call out the fire brigade. High maintenance, Gary called her.

It didn't quite go to plan. We got kind of side-tracked on the whole facial hair thing and rush hour trains are tricky – if I'd gone for the full on kiss and mistimed it as we clunked to a stop I might have been thrown into her lap, or broken her nose. Either way, I could have got arrested.

I kissed her, to shut her up, and because it actually was my stop and if I didn't hurry up I'd miss it. But I chickened out. Soft option. On the hand, which was a first. Christ, how corny. Pathetic. I don't know who was more surprised: her or me. Although an introduction to her knuckles might be a sign of things to come.

"See you tomorrow."

She gave a little smile, which could have meant "not if I see you first".

9:15 a.m.
Actually, I can't believe I did that. But I am not doing it again. Done. Finished. I'll either end up getting arrested for indecent assault, or she'll think I want her to have my babies. I didn't wait to find out how it went down, I just bolted for the exit. I broke every unwritten code of polite British commuting.

Incoming text. Gary Hopper: *"Well? Last week of target practice mate."*

Text to Gary Hopper: *"No. The women readers will hate it."*

Text from Gary Hopper: *"Bollocks."*

And when I glance up over the top of my laptop he's grinning across at me from his office (well, it isn't actually an office, it's a corner with filing cabinets round three sides to make him feel important), holding his cup of coffee up. I try not to smile in triumph, and fail.

"I knew it." Surprising how fast that man can move across the office when he wants. Talk about heat seeking missiles. With him, though, it's headline seeking.

"Sod off and leave me in peace. I've got a deadline."

"No way to talk to your boss." Gary leaned against my desk, like he intended to stay a bit.

"I am not going to pimp myself out for you with random women for a month."

"Not random. Just the one, and you've found one. So what's your problem?"

The man is an arsehole. That's my problem.

"And what if she doesn't turn up every day?"

"Pick a stand-in." He shrugged. "Plenty more fish in the sea, or birds on the train."

12:15 p.m.
Hit send on my latest "ManStyle" column and wonder how many men actually want to read about prostate checks. Enough to make a guy squirm just mentioning it. It's a bit like when women prattle on about having the dog neutered; I mean, it isn't something you need to talk about out loud, in public, is it?

Can't imagine that girl on the train mentioning dogs' bollocks out loud. Sweet. Soft skin. Unlike mine. I really could do with a shave. In fact, this week I should make the most of it. Go for suave and sophisticated.

Tuesday 28th October
Sophie
9 a.m.
Mr Darcy – sorry, Dave – wasn't there. OMG, one kiss and he's avoiding me. Everything they say about being too easy is true. I let him kiss me on the first date, well, first not-date. And now he's decided to take another train, or sit in another carriage. After months of togetherness it is over.

I did think about walking up and down to see if I could spot him. But that's stalkerish, and I'm not a stalker, just concerned.

We always sit in the same carriage. Travelling companions. I am doomed to a lonely spinster-dom. I am no longer Miss Bennet in a pretty bonnet, I am

Miss Havisham in a grubby wedding dress with no great expectations.

10:00 a.m.
Hannah looks more like Morticia every day. She is head to foot in black, probably because she thinks it is slimming, but instead she looks like a scary nun, or Morticia.

Except nuns do not wear heavy eyeliner and scarlet lips. Hannah has a boyfriend though, which makes her superior. I wonder if she bosses him around too? I really must read more of my book and find out how that works. Not sure there is any point now, we will never get to discussing whips and handcuffs.

10:15 a.m.
Am really not in the mood to write adverts. How many ways can you describe cute puppies? They are cute. Cars are easier, at least there are engine sizes and MoT certificates, but she has insisted I do "Pets and Livestock" today. Maybe I should get a cat.

I flicked through the photographs and was alarmed to see a picture of a Maine Coon that looked more like a bear than a cat. My flat isn't big enough for that size cat; I need something small, and preferably portable.

Cute kitten for sale, portable until full grown when wheelie case will be required.

Morticia frowns at me so I delete the words quick before she gets a chance to see them. She takes her job very seriously and might sack me.

I thought working in publishing would be more fun than this. I thought I'd meet hot actors (why can't Henry Cavill pop in for an interview and come and see us?) and get free clothes that the models had done shoots in, and designer make-up and handbags. I didn't think I would be restricted by character counts that would challenge even Twitter.

12:30 p.m.
Met Ellie for lunch. Told her about Mr Darcy.

"I've met a man."

She paused, mid bite of her healthy option wrap, then chewed rapidly like a rabbit to try and get rid of the healthy bits. Not easy, unless you want to risk choking. I understand now why rabbits need to twitch their noses as they eat.

"What, where, who?"

"On the train."

"Oh."

"What do you mean, oh?"

She took another bite and slowly chewed while she stared at me. "Sorry, Soph. It's just... on the train? I mean, who is he?"

"He's gorgeous, like... well, like..." I didn't want to share the Mr Darcy bit, she already thought I was mildly deranged. "Like Colin Firth," I said triumphantly. Close enough.

"Famous?"

"Well, no. But—"

"So, where did you go on your first date?"

"First date?" Some people always wanted to rush things. "We're at the chatting between stations bit."

"Oh." Ellie left the last bit of tortilla, as she

always did. It was her way of cutting down on carbs.

"I've known him for ages, longer than I knew Sam, in fact." I had, except at first I'd barely registered him as I was in the first stages of passionate love. Until I realised it wasn't.

"Ah, that man. Why don't you do the asking, a nudge in the right direction."

I picked up the last of my chips (healthy food that threatens to choke you isn't really my scene). "He wasn't there today."

"Look, I've got to go." She was wriggling her way out from behind the table. "I've got a meeting. But at least ask him his name, Soph."

"It's Dave. He wasn't there today, do you think it was the kiss? Did it put him off, one kiss?"

Ellie, half out of her seat, gave a little squeal and sat down again. "You've kissed? You didn't tell me that; you said you hadn't dated."

"We haven't, it was on the train. And it was only a little kiss." I'm not going to ruin things by admitting to the whole truth.

"Not even you can put a man off with one kiss, Soph. Hell, I'm going to be late. Text tomorrow, tell me if he kisses you again."

7 p.m.
He wasn't on the train, even though I don't normally see him in the evening. But he has to get home somehow, doesn't he? Have discovered another drawback to having a cat: no catflap. And as my apartment is on the third floor, small portable cat could suffer untimely death whilst chasing mice.

Not that I have mice.

11 p.m.
Eaten too much pizza, watching re-runs of *GBBO* and *Strictly Come Dancing*, think I will dream about sequin covered bread rolls. Or Pasha with pastry between his teeth, not a rose. No, strike that. Pasha would never do that.

Wednesday 29th October
Sophie
8.45 a.m.
Woohoo, he was on the train! He is not avoiding me, and is not dead. I was very tempted to ask him where the hell he'd been, but that would be mad womanish and inappropriate after only one kiss and no date. He was looking a bit dishevelled, but in a sexy way.

"How's things?" He sat down opposite me like we were friends, not one kiss associates.

"Good, thanks. You?"

"Sorry about the er—"

"No problem. I was…" *Worried* sounded like I am already serious, *concerned* sounds like I wanted to mother him. "…busy." Busy suits most occasions.

He frowned.

"Nothing serious, I hope?" I mean, it wasn't my business, but he looked really worried. Maybe he had some dreadful health problem, or he'd been off for a day going to a funeral. Or he'd split up with his girlfriend. "I don't want to be nosy, I mean, we hardly know each other, but sometimes it's better talking to somebody you don't know."

"Or kiss them."

"Oh."

"I hope you didn't mind me—"

"No, not at all." Oh no, he'll think I'm easy now.

"—Rushing off."

"It was your stop."

"I'm not usually that—"

"It was fine. I mean nice. I don't mind quick kisses."

"Rude. Look, I need to explain."

"No." This was getting worse by the minute. Though I didn't mean to shout that loud.

"Christ, this is me. Catch you later."

And he'd gone. Again. Bloody hell, I think the train driver must be watching us on CCTV and going as fast as he can.

"Shit." Mr Darcy was back. "Sorry."

And he kissed me, his rough cheek brushing against mine this time. No hands involved. Well, lips weren't all that involved either. Was that progress?

I rested my fingertips over the slight smart he'd left behind, sandpaper burn, as he'd bolted for the door.

I'd heard of speed dating but this was ridiculous.

Was he ever going to hang about long enough for a real snog? And when he was talking about moustaches and beards was it a warning that he never shaved?

Wednesday 29th October
Dave
8:45 a.m.

That didn't go well. She seemed to want to talk about something, which means I'm a git (not the new man I like to think). But I just wanted to explain, and find out if she really was game. And it's bloody typical that my mother chooses just the moment I get on the train to ring and want to discuss in a very loud voice how my father should go about finding his prostate. She'd heard it was important.

Which meant that by the time I'd sat down it was nearly time to get off (I was pretty damned certain the rest of the carriage did not want to hear about my father's nether regions, and my mother worked on the basis that I was as deaf as he was – turning down the volume on the phone just didn't seem to work at all).

So I had about two minutes left between pocketing my phone, finding my seat and having to get off the damned train again. And I am just not a quickie type of guy.

And when I glanced up as the train left the station, she was rubbing her cheek. Maybe I should have shaved the stubble, just left the moustache bit? Tomorrow is definitely clean-shaven day.

Bloody hell, it's nearly the end of the week. I need a Plan B.

Thursday 30th October
Sophie
7:30 a.m.

Morticia is a complete cow. I suggested that maybe I could do something slightly more challenging at work, seeing as I do actually have a degree, and she said I needed work experience. So she arranged for me to take notes at her 7 a.m. management meeting. She told them the meeting clashed with another one, and I would stand in, but I think she wanted a lie in. With her man. How am I supposed to get *my* man if I have to catch an early train?

Am worried that I'm getting a rash though, so the whole unshaved bit could be a problem. Maybe he is secretly a yeti, like a werewolf but not as extreme. What if I have a human hair allergy that I never knew about (male hair only, obviously, or I would be allergic to myself)?

Or maybe it's the cat in the flat next door? Except it's always been there, ever since I moved in, and I've not had a problem. Maybe I am just allergic to kissing good-looking men with sexy voices. Oh God, life is unfair. I meet my sex god and everything is conspiring against us. It is like Romeo and Juliet.

Thursday 30th October
Dave
8:45 a.m.
How could she not be on the train? I've been sitting opposite her every week day for the last few months, and when we need to talk she isn't there. Which screws up my whole Movember series for "ManStyle".

I'd decided exactly what I was going to say to her, explain the whole concept (even if Gary had told me not to).

After a furtive look round, I've realised that there isn't another bloody girl on the train I have any desire to kiss every day for a month.

Maybe I need to write about how sweaty Lycra cycle shorts can shoot your sperm count to kingdom come. Too predictable. Or list the top ten men who would still be with us if we'd had Movember earlier. Too depressing. Ten silliest stars with a moustache? Ten sexiest women with a moustache? Now I really am losing it.

Coffee, I need coffee.

10 a.m.

Think I've had too much coffee. I'm hallucinating, or Gary really is growing a moustache. He has plonked himself in front of the desk and won't go away.

"Is that real?"

"It is." He looks pleased with himself. "Thought I'd get a head start. Ha ha, head start."

"Very droll." How can it make a man look better? I will have to ask the train girl if there are any men who look better with a moustache or a beard. God, I don't even know her name, we only got as far as "stuck" and I've kissed her and already got her down for a snog a day marathon for a month. I'll be a major investor in mints.

If I ever see her again, that is. Maybe I've been stood up. Derailed. Tomorrow I must find her. Get things back on track. Hah! I'm beginning to sound as bad as Gary.

Friday 31st October
Sophie
9 a.m.

I am going to be famous, and I am going to be kissed. Lots. And for once I don't actually mind writing adverts out for dodgy plumbers or second-hand washing machines, because Mr Darcy and I have a deal. And he was so desperate to explain that he even missed his stop, and ended up walking me to work when I got off. I knew things were about to change when instead of sitting down, smiling and lifting his newspaper, he actually leant forward, elbows on knees and looked me straight in the eye.

"We need to talk. I'm sorry, but I've got an admission." He held up a hand to stop me interrupting (like I usually do – in fact, I wasn't going to interrupt, I was going to cough.) "No, let me tell you and then feel free to tell me to sod off."

I couldn't actually imagine wanting to tell him to sod off. He waited. I waited. Then he realised that I really wasn't going to stop him.

"The kiss…"

I opened my mouth, then changed my mind when he lifted a warning eyebrow – this man has animated body parts when he's talking. Which can be good.

"I did it for a reason." A reason? Not pure lust? "It's not that I don't find you attractive, you are, attractive. I mean, I do… find you. Hell, I fancy you, but I did have an ulterior motive for being so forward."

A shag? I live in hope.

"You've heard of Movember?"

I nodded encouragingly and racked my brain.

"Well, I'm going the full hog this year."

I nodded again, this time a little doubtfully.

"All the way."

"As in?"

"All month." He paused. "You don't know, do you?"

"Not a clue what you're talking about." There are times when ignorance is bliss, and times when it's bloody confusing. So I 'fessed up, and he explained. About raising awareness, and raising money, and how he wrote a daily column for a newspaper I'd actually heard of (I didn't admit to writing adverts for a free paper that not even my mother would own up to ever reading). He told me all about his 'ManStyle' column, and how they were running a daily highlight on Movember, and how his boss has come up with a twist of his own – writing about what women actually thought about it all. The moustaches, that is, not men's health.

"Strictly speaking I shouldn't be telling you this."

"Why not, is it a secret?" I'd heard about news-paper secrets, though obviously moustaches weren't normally considered top secret.

"I'm just supposed to see how you react as I get hairier, and write funny prose about it."

"Me? How I react?"

"Yes, you."

"But why would I react?" I suppose I might feel like slapping him if I have to watch him grope a different girl on the train every day. Or I could be mature and catch a different train.

"Because it's you I'd be kissing."

"Oh." It took a second to sink in. "Oh." I think I turned bright red, something had certainly heated up, and if it wasn't the train it had to be me.

"I mean, it's fine if you don't want to. I mean, if you don't fancy me at all."

"Oh, I do." I probably said that a bit fast, but he grinned.

"Really?"

"Really. Isn't this your stop?"

"Sod that. So you'll do it? I don't have to put your name in the paper."

"I mean, it is only because it's a good cause. I don't usually make a habit of kissing men on the train." But, boy, did I want to find out whether this one was a good kisser; I wanted to go straight to the real snogging stage if I were honest. I had been a bit concerned that we weren't going to get beyond a quick peck, but now I understood. He was saving the best bit for next week, and the week after. Maybe building to a dirty crescendo. To hell with the hairiness, and the stubble rash. I was game.

"So, you will?"

How could I resist? "What, for the whole of November?" Just to make the boundaries clear.

"The whole month, or I will have to tell the world that you abandoned me."

"I won't abandon you."

"What if it gets scratchy, or makes me look a muppet?"

"I'll give it a go. But I will have to tell you, about the muppet thing, if it happens."

"Fair deal. I sincerely hope you will."

I shouldn't look too eager. That will put him off.

Except he hasn't really got a choice, has he? And he is a sex god. And I am getting a bit addicted to him. But addiction is bad. I mean, what if giving him up is worse than giving up cigarettes? Or wine and chocolate?

"What are you thinking about?"

"Chocolate."

"So you don't actually want to? You can say, I'll understand." He looked seriously concerned.

But it was for a good cause. I am supporting men. I am a good citizen, almost a saint. "It is already getting a bit prickly."

"You're telling me." He looked rueful. And cute. Can you have a cute sex god? He is one of a kind.

"Maybe if you had the full works it would help."

"Sorry?"

I've shocked him again. "I mean a beard."

"It's Movember, as in Mo, for moustache."

"Ah yes, forgot that bit."

"Does it bother you?"

"I suppose it might grow on me."

"More like on me." He smoothed one fingertip along his top lip and grinned.

"It's a deal." I hold a hand out to shake, because it seems the polite thing to do.

"Oh, sod that. Let's start as we mean to go on."

And he does, with a great big proper snog. I needn't have worried after all. The man really can kiss. Ah well, needs must. So I got to grips with the situation, so to speak, I mean it is in a good cause.

It took quite a while to get untangled, then we got off the train and he walked me to work.

"Here, call me if you, er, have any questions." I stare at the business card. David Simmonds. He's a proper journalist. "Same time tomorrow?"

Oh, yes!

I'm being snogged for a good cause and I'm going to be in his diary, well, column, and I'm going to be famous. A bit like Bridget Jones....

The End

Zara Stoneley lives in deepest Cheshire surrounded by horses, dogs, cats and amazing countryside. When she's not visiting wine bars, artisan markets or admiring the scenery in her sexy high heels or green wellies, she can be found in flip-flops on the beach in Barcelona, or more likely sampling the tapas!

Best selling author Zara writes hot romance and bonkbusters. Her latest novel, *Stable Mates*, is a fun romp through the Cheshire countryside and combines some of her greatest loves – horses, dogs, hot men and strong women (and not forgetting champagne and fast cars). If you like Jilly Cooper and Fiona Walker, you'll love this!

She writes for Harper Collins and Accent Press.

Website: www.zarastoneley.com
FB: www.facebook.com/zarastoneley
Twitter: twitter.com/ZaraStoneley

Thank you for purchasing this anthology.

The HitLitPro authors, Candlelit Author Services and ThornBerry Publishing hope you have enjoyed reading these stories. Separate donations to the Movember Foundation can be made via uk.movember.com/donate.

www.ingramcontent.com/pod-product-compliance
Lightning Source LLC
Chambersburg PA
CBHW021147130626
46554CB00005B/1712